BEWARE THE BUTCHER BIRD

A Lucy Wayles Mystery

Lydia Adamson

SIGNET
Published by the Penguin Group
Penguin Books USA Inc., 375 Hudson Street,
New York, New York 10014, U.S.A.
Penguin Books Ltd, 27 Wrights Lane,
London W8 5TZ, England
Penguin Books Australia Ltd, Ringwood,
Victoria, Australia
Penguin Books Canada Ltd, 10 Alcorn Avenue,
Toronto, Ontario, Canada M4V 3B2
Penguin Books (N.Z.) Ltd, 182–190 Wairau Road,
Auckland 10, New Zealand

Penguin Books Ltd, Registered Offices:
Harmondsworth, Middlesex, England

First published by Signet, an imprint of Dutton Signet,
a division of Penguin Books USA Inc.

First Printing, June, 1997
10 9 8 7 6 5 4 3 2 1

PUBLISHER'S NOTE
This is a work of fiction. Names, characters, places, and incidents either
are the product of the author's imagination or are used fictitiously, and
any resemblance to actual persons, living or dead, events, or locales is
entirely coincidental.

Chapter 1

It was 6:31 P.M. on the second Tuesday in November. The first truly cold day of autumn.

I stood before the old wood-framed full-length mirror in my bedroom inspecting my appearance and knotting my tie—slowly, carefully.

I am hardly anyone's idea of a clotheshorse. But that night I was taking pains with my appearance. The tie I was fussing over was brand-new—only three hours old, in fact. I acquired it at one of the snootier men's stores on Madison Avenue. And I had spent an absolutely outrageous sixty-eight dollars on it. Plus tax. All to impress my lady love, Miss Lucy Wayles.

It *was* a lovely tie, if a little audacious. Deep brown silk with lighter brown herons dancing down its length in a pretty pattern.

Yes, I simply had to impress Lucy, and goodness knows I'd have gone a lot further than purchasing an overpriced cravat to do it.

When I was satisfied that the knot was perfect, I stepped back to take in my total image.

Oh.

I was still rather short. Still a geriatric Romeo. I had not been transformed into a matinee idol.

No matter. I felt wonderful anyway. I was escorting Lucy to a gala dinner that night. All our bird-watching colleagues would be in attendance as well. It was going to be a grand evening. And why not? The morning had been just as grand.

Lucy had led us into the park at 7:00 A.M., as usual—"us" being Olmsted's Irregulars, bird-watchers without peer.

Actually, we were not an old, established bird-watching group. We were relatively new. Lucy Wayles, the president and founder, had split us off from the parent group—the Central Park Bird Watchers—because of, as she put it, "severe ideological differences."

In fact, Lucy had been asked in less than polite terms to leave the parent group a little over a year ago. She had been arrested for holding up traffic on the 59th Street Bridge during her daring high-wire rescue of a wayward tufted duck. But for her efforts, the frightened creature would surely have frozen to death. It had been something of a media event. Lucy even made the six o'clock news.

But the Central Park Bird Watchers had found her actions less than dignified. Lucy's heroics were definitely not the kind of attention the group appreciated. Some of the group members had words with Lucy. And needless to say, she had some choice words for them. One thing led to another. And the end result was the founding of our little splinter group.

Olmsted's Irregulars (named, of course, after the genius who designed Central Park) originally consisted of Lucy, myself, Peter Marin, John Wu, Emma Pip, and Beatrice Plumb.

Alas, two of these individuals were no longer among our number. Indeed, they were now doing their birding from prison yards upstate, after a most complicated series of events led them to participate in a gruesome murder—all of which I have detailed elsewhere.

At any rate, the Irregulars had recently picked up a new member: Willa Wayne, a young woman—forty being quite young by my standards—who gave every indication of being a sterling addition to our group. She was lively and intelligent and very pretty and, apparently, quite well off. It seemed that every garment she owned, even the short pants and rugby shirts she often wore for bird-watching, had been purchased at the very poshest of the designer boutiques in town.

Ms. Wayne had not exactly been forthcoming about her personal life: she told us that she was married to a violinist with the New York Philharmonic, but as yet she had not disclosed his name.

Our first stop that morning was the reservoir.

Nothing unusual there—laughing gulls and ducks—from canvasbacks to greater and lesser scaups to buffleheads.

In a little while we moved on to the Ramble—that expanse of wooded beauty where the city and all its cares seemed simply to fade away. You could not glimpse a single skyscraper or hear a single taxicab's horn from the depths of the Ramble. It was like a country glade right in the middle of Manhattan.

By night, of course, the story was quite different. Things went on in that sylvan glade that were the stuff of nightmares. Things that only the birds would know about.

It was there in the Ramble that we came upon three red-bellied woodpeckers cavorting on a very old pin oak.

Not red-*headed* woodpeckers, mind you! These were red-*bellied* woodpeckers, which are rare in Central Park. And they were keeping up a fearsome racket that sounded very like the mad mariachi section in a Latin mambo band.

It sounded something like:

chuh . . . chuc-chuh . . .

chow-chow . . . cherr-cherr

And sometimes:

chawh-chawh!!

They were also making all kinds of strange moves in syncopation with their song: raising their crests, spreading wings and tails, bowing. It was something to see!

Their backs and rumps were conspicuously barred in black and white—transversely. Their underparts were gray. Their wings were spotted or barred with white. And what appeared to be their vaunted red bellies were really only reddish tinges on their abdomens.

I thought I heard John Wu mumble something.

"What was that?" I asked him.

"An irregular wanderer," John announced scornfully, lip curled.

He was referring to the birds, surely, not me. And I assumed he meant that the red-bellied woodpecker does not have a regular migration pattern.

Well, John was seldom wrong about such things. But so what? Why was the humble woodpecker's migration pattern a subject for his contempt?

John was a fairly strange bird himself, but it would never occur to me to question or challenge him. His knowledge of the avian world was vast, while mine was minuscule. And he was a respected investment counselor working in a dynamic business atmosphere, while I was a superannuated retired physician whose specialty had been research on the virus that causes the common cold. Not terribly glamorous, is it?

I turned my attention back to the dancing birds. John Wu's scorn notwithstanding, I rather admired them for their irregularity; but, at my age, the incongruities in life seemed much more interesting than the predictable patterns.

We watched a while longer. As I looked at the woodpeckers, I began to feel an almost overwhelming sadness.

You see, they reminded me of our two incarcerated comrades (they had a coconspirator in their crimes who wasn't a bird-watcher).

The birds had discovered a cache of seeds and now looked like convicts in the prison yard haggling over a smoke.

I cast a quick and furtive glance at burly Peter Marin. Apparently he had not picked up on the connection. Still, I tried to keep an eye on poor Peter. He had been devastated by the whole affair. I honestly doubt that he will ever recover from it.

By and by, the woodpeckers left us.

During our morning break one of those inevitable arguments broke out. Such altercations are unfailingly heated, but at the same time they seem to invigorate the arguing birders no end. In truth, bird-watchers would rather fight than eat.

This time the argument was between Peter and the new member, Willa Wayne.

Willa said, speaking of the departed woodpeckers, "Those birds are obvious psychotics. Obvious. This is not the season for courtship rituals."

Whereupon Peter Marin replied, "I beg to differ with you. That was not courtship behavior we just witnessed."

"Are you blind? Of course it was," Willa countered indignantly. She had a long, thin face, and when she turned her black dagger eyes upon you it was as if you were being pinned to velvet like a prize butterfly.

"The courtship behavior of the red-bellied woodpecker," Peter spat out venomously, "is characterized by mutual tapping and reverse mounting. Period. It's textbook stuff, madam."

"Does anybody have any salt?"

It was Lucy who had interrupted the fight with that innocuous question. She was holding a shelled hard-boiled egg.

We all began to search our backpacks for salt.

And the argument was forgotten.

Once again, Lucy had displayed her leadership qualities.

Yes, all in all, a very good morning.

When I finished dressing, I walked into Duke's bedroom to get his opinion.

No, I do not have a roommate. Not exactly. Let me explain: Duke is a three-legged pit bull who—how shall I put it?—came into my life recently.

He was foisted off on me by Lucy and her crazy down-home Aunt Hattie—who is wont to wander around Manhattan with a loaded shotgun.

Duke doesn't like me particularly, but I value his opinions, when he cares to express them—which is not often.

The beast was in his favorite spot, on the rug, surrounded by dozens of rawhide bones, which Lucy keeps sending him.

Duke likes holding one of them in his teeth when we go for a walk.

People on the street, seeing this pit bull hip-hopping along on three legs with a bone in his jaws, just don't know what to say or do or think.

One lady walked over to me, keeping clear of Duke, handed me a five-dollar bill, and whispered: "Why don't you buy this poor dog a real bone?"

I stood in the middle of Duke's room, striking a pose with my coat draped over one arm. "Well, what do you think?"

The beady-eyed bugger groaned, got up, and hobbled around to the other side of the bed, out of sight.

I could hear him plop down again.

"Thank you, Duke," I said pleasantly. "That will be all for now."

I took the elevator down, nodded good evening to the doorman, and headed toward the Hilton. It was a short walk from my 57th Street apartment to the hotel.

I looked at my watch. It was 7:03.

Lucy had set the time of arrival for 7:15. We were all to meet then, across from the Hilton, in the small park at 54th Street.

Lucy had said a preliminary meeting was necessary because the award dinner might become so boring so fast that a rational escape plan must be drawn up.

Why the dinner? And what was the award? All the Irregulars had asked those questions when Lucy first informed us of the festivities.

A number of environmental and wildlife groups—including Audubon, Sierra Club, and Nature Conservancy—had formed a kind of consortium to create the Conservationist of the Year medal. Tonight would be the first presentation of the honor, and it was planned that the award banquet be a yearly event.

The medal itself—we'd seen a photograph of it on the invitation that Lucy had received—featured a bold design: a naked man and woman holding hands while riding a huge Galapagos tortoise.

And the individual whom the consortium had selected to receive the first medal was none other than Jack Wesley Carbondale, America's most famous living bird artist and the author of the renowned *Carbondale's Field Guides to the Birds*.

Even Lucy, who received the tickets in the mail, out of the blue, did not know why she was being invited.

The best explanation she could think of was simply that Carbondale remembered her from the archives.

Lucy Wayles, before she became a gentlewoman birder, was director and head librarian of the world-famous Archives of Urban Natural History, now part of the Museum of Natural History.

During her tenure there, Carbondale and his assistants had used the archives when preparing new editions of their famous field guides.

Anyway, the invitation could not be refused.

As Peter Marin, himself a rather successful commercial artist, put it: "Is there really any bird-watcher alive who doesn't love the drawings of Carbondale? I doubt it. Academics love him. Avant-garde sculptors love him. Old-lady watercolorists love him. Tattoo artists love him. Even dead cubists love him."

"Stop carrying on," John Wu had cautioned. It was true: Peter always tended to extremes.

I turned east on 55th Street and entered the park. The weather had softened. It was now an Indian summer evening.

I saw them before they saw me. All my comrades, standing together in the early evening light. Probably they were expecting me to approach via 54th Street.

I took in the whole scene, genuinely moved. The bustling crowds. My friends and colleagues waiting for me in the park. The old-fashioned street lamps raining soft light down on the passersby. The stately hotel across the way, doormen all in braid and snap-brimmed caps. Even the classic New York frankfurter cart at the curb with its fine yellow umbrella had taken on a romantic glow.

Peter Marin was wearing an extremely

strange-looking gold corduroy suit that was too small for him. It was, however, a distinct improvement over his ubiquitous overalls. I am about as tolerant of the eccentricities of others as a man my age can be, but it had always puzzled me why Peter Marin chose to walk around looking like Li'l Abner.

John Wu was dressed in his usual cool, anonymously elegant gray. He was one of those people born to wear clothes and wear them well. I had trouble imagining him unclad, even as a newborn.

Willa Wayne might have just emerged from Monsieur Givenchy's salon. Her gown was classic fire-engine red, with a daring, low-plunging back that stopped a thumbnail short of . . . well, one could almost see . . . well, I hadn't seen a dress like that in many a year . . . not since that film in the 1970s, *Shampoo*, where the sight of Julie Christie's backless dress had triggered an asthmatic condition I had not even known I had before that instant.

And as for my Lucy? Oh, that was another story altogether! She took my breath away.

Lucy had allowed her usually short-cropped white hair to grow out. It was now long enough, in fact, for her to braid. And that night it was piled high on her head, in the style of Kitty, the saloon girl in those old western movies.

She wore a long black dress with a high waist, and over it, draped around her shoulders, was one of her short denim jackets—this one rose-colored. She wore tiny black pearl earrings.

And madame's slippers . . . I looked down to see that she was wearing her ugly old rubberized birder boots.

Well, Lucy always made a statement.

My heart was bumping with joy. Lord, she was beautiful. Boots and all.

I called hello to the assembled and they turned as one.

"It's about time, Markus Bloch," Lucy said when she saw me.

At first I didn't catch the little smile playing at the corners of her mouth. I was too busy gazing at the little pink spots she had rouged on her cheeks.

"But I'm not late, Lucy," I replied defensively.

She was staring at me. In fact, they all were. I felt a bit self-conscious.

Finally, her face broke into a wonderful

smile and she said, "I declare, Markus Bloch! We are quite the dandy this evening!"

I wanted to purr.

But then John Wu said, "Don't take what I'm about to say the wrong way, Markus. But that thing around your neck must be the ugliest tie I have ever seen in my life."

Willa, obviously stricken, tried to soothe my hurt feelings: "But the fabric is interesting, Markus. Highly . . . unusual silk."

"It most certainly is," Lucy interjected and then, without skipping a beat, continued with, "Let's bite the apple," meaning, I supposed, that we should get down to business.

I detected in her "bite" a hint of Southern accent. But not the deep, broad Tennessee/Virginia eruption that came when she was angry.

No, this was just a smattering of it—to get our attention.

From where we stood, we could see the award dinner guests entering the hotel on the 54th Street side. Cabs and limos pulled up. There were even a few photographers snapping photos, because a deputy mayor and a famous Broadway personality were co-masters of ceremonies.

Lucy said, "I think we must commit to at

least three. In other words, we can't even think of leaving before three speakers have gotten up and sat down again. Agreed?"

We all agreed.

Lucy continued. "Now there'll be hors d'oeuvres and drinks when we walk in. But the dinner won't be served until after all the speakers are finished and the award has been presented. Can we wait that long? Will the boredom crush us? Here's what I propose. After the third speaker, anyone who thinks an exit is warranted taps his glass twice with a fork. When three of us have tapped in confirmation, we all leave. And Markus will take us to a lovely restaurant in his neighborhood. Agreed?"

"How many taps of the fork?" Peter asked.

"Two."

"Got it. Two taps. Three agreements. Does it have to be a glass?"

"As you wish, Peter," Lucy said kindly. "Tap on anything you can find."

"Are you sure we will be seated at the same table?" asked Willa.

"Of course," Lucy said. "They wouldn't dare split up Olmsted's Irregulars."

Lucy often made strange statements. Strangely

optimistic ones. I was sure there couldn't have been more than two out of the five hundred guests and officials of the awards dinner who had ever even heard of Olmsted's Irregulars.

Five abreast, we started across the traffic-choked street toward the hotel entrance.

Suddenly a shadow crossed my eyes.

It was very quick. A flash. Something dark.

Then I heard a savage thud.

Willa screamed.

The sidewalk shuddered beneath our feet.

And a fountain seemed to emerge out of nowhere . . . a bubbling red geyser.

Cars screeched to a stop. People froze in their tracks.

And then the screaming really began. The whole block was echoing with cries and shrieks.

Someone had leaped from a high window at the Hilton.

He had landed on the umbrella of the frankfurter stand.

Impaled!

I felt someone pulling my arm. It was Lucy.

She quickly rounded up all the stunned Irregulars and marched us into the hotel.

Once inside, she counted heads as if we were children on a grade school outing.

I adjusted my tie. That's right. After the horror I had just seen, I could think of nothing else to do.

Lucy walked over to me and caressed my face.

"Are you all right, Markus?"

"I am a physician," I heard myself say, my voice like something from beyond the grave. "Certainly I'm all right. I was trained to deal with trauma."

"You don't look it," she said.

"It happened right in front of me!" I exploded. "*Splat!*"

She trapped my gesticulating hands and stilled them. "Oh, Markus, Markus."

"What?"

"Beware the butcher bird, Markus," she said softly.

"What the hell does that mean?"

She smiled her cryptic smile and headed into the party area, gently pulling me after her.

John Wu, cool and composed as you please, whispered from behind me, into my ear, "The butcher bird is a common name for the northern shrike. It impales its victims on thorns."

Thank you, John! For nothing, as usual.

About five minutes later, as the delicious miniature pizzas I am so fond of were being served by tall, gaunt waiters, we learned that the flying object had been Jack Wesley Carbondale.

Chapter 2

Usual time; usual place. We met the following morning at seven just inside the park at East 90th and 5th Avenue, in front of the statue of a long-dead mayor.

But the moment I arrived with my trusty navy surplus binocs swung rakishly around my neck I had a feeling there wouldn't be a usual birding adventure that morning.

Everyone was shaky and ashen—even Lucy. Obviously the shock had been delayed for twelve hours; because we had all been positively jaunty, indeed heroic, after the tragedy, even though poor Carbondale had been impaled right in front of us.

Of course, the awards dinner had been canceled as soon as the identity of the jumper was revealed. But Olmsted's Irregulars had then repaired en masse to a chophouse, whereupon we ate and drank and chatted as if nothing really bad had happened—just another butcher bird victim on a thorn, as Lucy, a little tipsy, had noted, continuing her ornithological symbolism. Oh! It made me love her even more. Sometimes she was so damned cosmic! In fact, I stopped drinking right after that for fear of unbridled passion.

But now, on this chilly morning, we stood in a circle of gloom.

Only John Wu seemed to have his mind on birding. Or rather, his mind was on scoring points against Willa Wayne concerning the behavior of the red-bellied woodpecker.

In fact, he started right in, his mellifluous drone like a pedantic sledgehammer. But his words did not go to the heart of the previous day's argument—whether or not the woodpeckers were performing courtship rituals out of season. No, John was merely showing off his knowledge.

"There has long been a controversy," he said, "about the red-bellied woodpecker in Florida, where it is also called the orange sapsucker. Some claim the bird destroys the orange trees by boring and sucking as well as eating the oranges on the tree. Others disagree. They say the woodpecker only eats fallen fruit after it has decayed slightly. Ah, yes, it is a point of contention."

There was no response by Willa.

John then added another tidbit: "In the northern part of its range, ants make up about eleven percent of its diet."

"I think the figure is closer to twelve percent," said Peter Marin, twitting Wu.

"What the hell does this have to do with the woodpeckers we saw yesterday?" Willa asked through gritted teeth.

Lucy terminated this rather ludicrous conversation abruptly. She dropped her small knapsack onto the ground, opened it, and began a feverish hunt inside of it, as if she were looking for buried treasure.

Then she pulled out, triumphantly, part of a newspaper page.

"Did any of you read Maccann's column this morning?" she asked, displaying the paper for all to see.

Each of us shook his head in turn. Birdwatchers rarely read the tabloids. The *Times* is the only public source for birder information, and even so, such news is only occasional. Six weeks ago, for example, the *Times* did report the sighting of a rare gull on the Connecticut shore.

"I shall read it to you," Lucy announced.

"You mean during our break?" Peter Marin asked.

"No! Now," Lucy replied. Then she added: "I think there will be no outing today."

We stared at our fearless leader, dumbstruck. It was one thing to intuit, as I had, that we would be less than vigorous in our ornithological pursuits that morning, given the aftershocks of Carbondale's hurtling body.

But to suspend operations? That was unthinkable for any reason short of all-out, worldwide, thermonuclear war.

"First we need some coffee . . . all of us . . . now," Lucy said to her flock.

Now here was another brazen flouting of tradition. We never ate or drank anything from the moment of assembly to our break several hours later.

Worse than the flouting was the fact that I was the official gofer of Olmsted's Irregulars, as well as being in charge of the garbage bag.

But there was no arguing with legally con-

stituted authority, particularly since that authority—Lucy Wayles—was the only reason I
was in the group. I was there to court her and
win her.

Off I trudged to Lexington Avenue and then
back with assorted coffees, teas, and low-fat
muffins.

Lucy led us up the slope, and we stood
only a few feet from the cinder track circling
the reservoir. The joggers whizzed past us.

Lucy began to read from the ripped-out
column of newsprint:

"Jack Wesley Carbondale, the world-famous
nature artist best known for his vivid bird
portraiture, killed himself last night moments
before he was to attend an awards banquet in
his honor at the New York Hilton.

"Authorities describe his death as 'a classic
suicide.' Carbondale undressed in his room,
1502, carefully folded his clothing, emptied
his pockets and laid the contents on a table,
cut up his credit cards, balled up his socks,
lined up his shoes under the bed, and jumped
from his hotel window.

"Apparently Carbondale had been drinking before his leap to death. Found in the

room were a half-finished bottle of Courvoisier cognac and a single paper cup.

"No suicide note was discovered. But on the wall he had scribbled with a thick crayon: NO REMORSE!

"His wife, Bo Carbondale, herself a celebrated artist, had left the room a few hours earlier to meet friends.

"Mrs. Carbondale told the police that the 68-year-old painter had been depressed and exhausted as of late but not physically ill.

"Carbondale's suicide is made even more poignant by the fact that he had just delivered to his publisher new drawings for the forthcoming sixth edition of his classic *Field Guide to Birds of the Mid-Atlantic Region*."

Lucy looked up.

"That is all I shall read," she declared. "The columnist goes on to talk about aging and emotional instability and how Carbondale was a perfect example of why depression in the aging male must be treated quickly. None of this really concerns us, does it now? There are no aging males in the Irregulars."

We didn't know if she was making a joke. Not one of us laughed.

She folded the piece of newsprint carefully,

fastidiously, as if it were the beginning or end of some original project.

"So?" Peter Marin queried.

Lucy hoisted her backpack. The folded newsprint remained in her hand. "Does nothing bother you people about what I just read?" she asked, a bit testily. My, she was lovely on the reservoir slope that autumn morning. I had a sense that despite her pique all was right with the world.

John Wu's eyes were now fixed on a point past Lucy's shoulder, on the cinder track. I knew what he was thinking: Is that female ring-necked duck still at the reservoir? What about the lesser scaups? When are we going to get on with our business? Doesn't this lady know that the deeper we get into autumn bird-watching, the more intense we have to become?

I even caught a little gleam of affection for John in Willa's eyes as she, too, picked up on his gaze.

"What about you, Markus?"

Uh-oh.

"Yes, Lucy?"

"You were a physician and a scientist and a

researcher. A man of reason. Wasn't Spinoza your hero? What think you, Markus?"

"Well . . . aah . . . I think it was a fine column. At least what you read of it. As for depression in the aging—"

She cut me off with a quick movement of her fine-boned right hand. "May I continue? At the risk of appearing arrogant? Now, we all know why Carbondale achieved fame and fortune—his field guides are unique in modern times. Why? Because he still worked in watercolors. And he was accurate. So every time you open a Carbondale guide you are treated to a rendition of, say, the red phalarope that is both stunning and real. Why was Carbondale so accurate? Because he did his preliminary drawings in the field. He was a field artist. He went to the mountains, the swamps, the forests. He lived in tents. He made his morning coffee on an open fire."

She paused and looked around. No one knew what to say, how to respond.

"In other words, my friends," Lucy said, "any man who spent that much time camping out in hostile terrain would never 'ball' his socks before jumping out of a window. You don't 'ball' your socks in unfamiliar terrain.

Too inviting for snakes and scorpions. You just leave them as they lay. No. Jack Wesley Carbondale did not 'ball' those socks."

Her revelation was greeted by stunned silence. After a minute, she smiled sadly and said, "I am very weary. Go on without me. I am going home to sleep."

And then, without another word, she walked away. Just walked away. Can you imagine that! I mean, it had never happened before in the history of Olmsted's Irregulars.

What a bind I was in. After a few moments of grumbling and muttering, the group headed off into the park. Lucy headed the other way, out of the park. I stood where I was. No one had given me any instructions at all.

Did Lucy want me to go with her? Or with the group? What had gotten into that woman? The man had jumped out a window, balled socks or not.

My heart spoke. I ran after Lucy, who had already made her way out of the park. I caught up with her as she was crossing Madison Avenue.

"What are you doing here, Markus?"

"Going with you?"

"Do your duty!" she barked.

"Which is?"

She pointed imperiously toward the park.

There was no dealing with Lucy when she became imperious. I ambled back into the park and found the Irregulars an hour later on the west side of the reservoir. They had still not located the ring-necked duck.

I spent the rest of the day and evening in a daze. At eleven o'clock I retired without even saying good night to the Duke in his own bedroom.

The phone rang at two minutes past midnight, waking me from a deep sleep.

It was Lucy. She calmly said, "Please inform the others that I won't be there tomorrow morning."

"What is it, Lucy?" I asked. "Are you ill?"

"No, not ill. I'm fine, Markus."

"Then why are you avoiding us . . . me?"

"Just some solitude, Markus."

"But you'll think better with me around. Come to breakfast with me. Or lunch. Or anything. This isn't right, Lucy. I'm worried about you. I'm lonesome. I miss you."

"You just saw me this morning, Markus."

"Yes, but it wasn't . . . us . . . together. Like we usually are."

"You are a fantasizer, Markus Bloch," she said and hung up.

I went into the Duke's bedroom, just for the company. The beast was on the rug, on his back, snoring gently, all three legs up in the air. It dawned on me that I was *his* pet, rather than the other way around. Forgive me, Spinoza—I have become a total fool!

Lucy appeared in the park two mornings later. She acted as if nothing whatsoever had happened. It was a cold morning. A bit damp. The sun appeared to be unreliable.

"Are we ready?" was all she said. And then she marched us off, not even waiting for an answer. By the southerly direction we were taking I perceived she was leading us toward the primeval Ramble. That made ornithological sense. The denser the cover in autumn, the more rewarding the catch—if any.

But we hadn't gone more than a hundred yards when Lucy made a precipitous turn and led us *under* one of the cast-iron bridges that cross the bridle path between East Drive and the cinder path of the reservoir.

"We needn't go any farther. Here is fine," Lucy announced.

"Fine for what?" a nervous Peter Marin asked.

"What if a horse and rider appear?" Willa Wayne said worriedly.

Lucy gave her one of those "oh, ye of faint heart" looks and then proceeded with the matter at hand. "Jack Wesley Carbondale will be buried in a few hours. In Connecticut. I am here to tell you and prove to you that they are burying a murder victim, not a suicide."

"Ladies and gentlemen! The princess of balled socks!" John Wu shouted mockingly.

Lucy ignored him, except to say quietly, "We are beyond socks now."

Then she motioned for all of us to come closer.

We formed a little circle around her, right there, on the riding path, underneath the bridge.

A passing tourist might have thought to himself, Ah, a group of bird-watchers stopping for a moment of prayer before they set out. Maybe they are praying for a rare sighting.

Another passerby, one with bad eyesight,

might have thought, Goodness! A group of blue jays mobbing an owl.

The latter observation was actually closer to the reality, since Lucy Wayles often claimed she had been an owl in a previous incarnation. The problem was, she was unsure as to just what kind of owl. Sometimes a lovely mouse-killing barn owl. Sometimes a cuddly burrowing owl. And sometimes she was the Great Horned Owl.

"Come a little closer," Lucy urged us.

"What is this—some kind of dance?" Peter complained.

"Someone has to keep a lookout for horses," Willa insisted.

We moved closer. I noticed that Lucy was not wearing her usual neo-hippie birding outfit. That is, except for her birder boots, she was wearing garments I had never seen before on any of our expeditions: baggy corduroy slacks, a soccer-type pullover, and a new black-and-white band around her forehead. All the others were dressed in their traditional birder garb. Big, red-haired Peter had on his trusty Li'l Abner overalls with the frayed cross straps. Willa was wearing one of her favorite boutique birder outfits—pastel

Bermuda shorts with matching shirt and Argyle socks. And fastidious John Wu was dressed in his usual gray pullover and slacks, as if he were going to a tennis match.

Standing so close to her this way triggered my old chagrin. I knew it was a trifle silly, but there it was. You see, Lucy is taller than I. The circle highlighted that fact. And deep in my heart I had always harbored the suspicion that my courtship of her was hindered by this disparity in height.

"I want you all to close your eyes," Lucy said.

We did so, some a bit reluctantly.

"Now imagine you are standing on the east side of Sixth Avenue, between Fifty-third and Fifty-fourth streets. You are looking west across the avenue, at the Hilton.

"What do you see? A dark slab of a building rising straight up. But then you notice something else. The slab takes up only three quarters of the space. On the downtown side of the hotel is a smaller, three-story building that houses the garage.

"Open your eyes and listen. I spent all day yesterday doing some very interesting research. It seems that there have been eleven leaping suicides at the Hilton over the past fifteen years.

"All but two occurred on the south side of the hotel.

"Why? Quite simple. If you check into a hotel to kill yourself, you surely don't want to jump directly onto the street. You may land on a passerby and kill him or her. What's more, the passerby just might break your fall—and you'll end up killing an innocent person while you survive.

"So you make sure and jump from the south side of the tower, landing on top of the three-story attached garage.

"Now, if Carbondale, of all people, had wanted to jump, he'd have leapt from the south side of the building, not the north. But he didn't jump. He was thrown!"

"What if Carbondale didn't go there to commit suicide?" John Wu protested. "What if he just had too much of that brandy, became despondent, and jumped on the spur of the moment?"

"Unlikely," Lucy replied dismissively.

"Why don't you go to the police?" Peter Marin asked, tugging at one strap of his coveralls.

"The men in blue are hawks, Peter. They hunt and strike. Which is what they're supposed to do. I think what is required here is not a hawk but a hummingbird. A hoverer."

I wanted to say something intelligent, but I couldn't think of anything. So all I managed was, "Yes. Hovering is good."

It was such a stupid remark that no one even bothered to look my way.

"So," Lucy continued, "given these facts, I propose that Olmsted's Irregulars meet an hour later tomorrow morning, at a different location."

"At the Hilton?" John responded.

"No," said Lucy. "At the corner of Houston Street and the Bowery."

"What are we meeting there for?" Peter demanded.

"Trust me, Peter."

"But there are no birds down there," Willa said.

Lucy arched her eyebrows. She brought forth her Southern accent. "Now, how do we know that? I believe Houston Street runs from rivah to rivah. The Hudson on the west, the East Rivah on the east. How do we know it's not an autumn flyway with terns and gulls and petrels and geese?"

Geese! Geese on the Bowery!

We were dumbstruck. Had Lucy Wayles gone round the bend?

She gave us our final instructions for the morrow: "If any of y'all have a Carbondale field guide . . . carry it!"

Chapter 3

So there we all were, the full complement of Olmsted's Irregulars, in full birding regalia, standing on the southeast corner of Houston and the Bowery at 8:00 A.M.

We were not alone.

Swirls, flocks, bevies of homeless people walked to and fro, seeking the shelters and soup kitchens all along the Bowery. They stared at us with genuine curiosity.

"They think we're DEA agents," noted John Wu.

"More likely they think we're lost bird-watchers," Peter Marin corrected.

Willa said nothing. She was scanning the sky with her mother-of-pearl binoculars, purchased at a Madison Avenue store that caters to rich hikers. She was looking for that mythical autumnal flyway that Lucy had suggested might exist on Houston Street between the two . . . rivahs.

Then our leader called out, "Follow me!"

We did. Across the wide street and south, past several bustling establishments that sold restaurant equipment and piled their excess merchandise on the street.

We stopped suddenly at the door between two such establishments. There seemed to be eleven bells on the door. Lucy turned, smiled at us, as if to assure us she knew exactly what she was doing, turned back, and, using both hands, rang ten out of the eleven bells.

Willa nudged me. Her pretty face had a very serious and concerned cast. "Is it true, Markus," she whispered, "that Lucy once asked you to follow her into the eye of Hurricane Hugo and all you said was, 'Should I bring an umbrella?' "

I wouldn't dignify the comment with a reply. One or another of the Irregulars was always giving me gentle digs about my affection for Lucy. Ah! True love is a cross to bear.

Three bells rang back. Lucy smiled again, as if to say, here's the proof that we are expected.

We entered the loft building and began our ascent of the steep, winding, dark stairs.

"We are going to the top," Lucy called out merrily.

Initially I was directly behind her, but as we climbed, the others passed me by, one by one, until, at the end of the ascent, I was half a landing behind and breathing heavily.

But I did hear Peter Marin exclaim, "My God! An old-fashioned artist's studio! I haven't been in a place like this for years."

When at last I reached the others, I could appreciate his outburst. Spread out from the landing was a huge high-ceilinged and many-windowed room filled with an assortment of clutter—from paint boxes to cutting tables to standing palettes to stacks of drawing pads and canvases and oak tag. And then there were files—oh, so many files.

Four people were present in the studio. They ignored us completely.

Three of the four appeared to be in an absolute frenzy—rushing back and forth, yelling at one another, cursing, upending items. It was obvious that they were searching for something.

Lucy pointed to the fourth person in the studio, a middle-aged woman with close-cropped brown hair, who was dressed in a denim jumpsuit. She was seated on a chair, calmly watching the circus of movement going on around her. The only sign of agitation that she exhibited was her compulsive touching of one of her pendent earrings.

"That is Jack Wesley Carbondale's widow. The artist Bo Carbondale," Lucy said in a dramatic whisper.

She headed toward Mrs. Carbondale, motioning that we should follow. When we reached the seated woman, Lucy first stated her own name and then formally introduced us, en masse, as a birder group.

Then she presented us individually, pronouncing each of our names distinctly and giving the widow time to nod courteously at each person as his or her name was called.

"We are here to offer our condolences. Your husband was a giant," Lucy said.

Bo Carbondale smiled. I could see immediately that this woman was heavily sedated. Why shouldn't she be? She had buried her husband only the day before.

Bo shook hands with each of us and thanked us in a slow and benevolent manner.

Then she called a halt to the crazed proceedings of her colleagues long enough to introduce us to each of them.

She extended her palm toward a tall, craggy man wearing unlaced sneakers. "This is Maurice Drabkin. He's a fine artist. He helped Jack a great deal."

Next she gestured to a very thin blond woman wearing a Johns Hopkins sweatshirt over her jeans. "Norma Hennion, these are Olmsted's Irregulars. Norma," she explained to us, "basically writes the guidebooks."

"And this—" Bo said, her voice quavering just slightly—"is a dear friend, Don Franco. Jack's researcher."

The trio greeted us hastily and then resumed their activity.

"What, if I may ask, are they looking for?" Lucy said.

It certainly was a logical question. The three people seemed to get more frantic with every passing second. They were literally ripping the loft apart. It was very disconcerting to watch.

But Bo Carbondale seemed merely amused.

"Well," she began her answer to Lucy's question, "Ann Nautica called, you see. She was Jack's editor. It seems when he delivered the manuscript he forgot to bring the gull plates. They're just not there. And we can't find them anywhere. Of course stats were made. But . . . the stats have vanished as well."

After her explanation she settled back in, that faraway smile on her lips. "It was so nice of you to come here," Bo said to Lucy after a minute. "What did you say your name was again?"

"Wayles. Lucy Wayles."

Lucy began to signal us surreptitiously, hands behind her back, that she wished to speak to Mrs. Carbondale alone.

Peter, John, and Willa discreetly moved back a few feet.

I remained where I was. After all, hadn't Lucy used the image of a hovering hummingbird? Well, I was hovering. And I heard the entire strange conversation that took place between her and the widow Carbondale:

"I wish to bring up a sensitive topic, Mrs. Carbondale," Lucy began.

"Oh? By all means, do, Miss Wayles. I have always been partial to sensitive topics."

"To be blunt, I do not think your husband committed suicide."

Bo Carbondale didn't blink an eye. "I assure you, we buried him yesterday, Miss Wayles. In the ground. In Connecticut."

"Of course. I mean, I think he was murdered. Someone threw your husband out of that window."

"Why would you think that? Why would anyone want to kill Jack?"

In reply, Lucy gave a concise résumé of her "evidence," including the balled-socks theory, and the statistical data on the side of the building favored by Hilton leapers, and why one side was preferable over the other.

When she was finished, a smiling Bo Carbondale leaned forward and took Lucy's hand. "You seem like a very nice person, Miss Wayles. Believe me, the moment I hear from Jack I'll ask him who killed him. I've been expecting him to contact me shortly, to let us know where he put those gull plates. Now I have *two* questions to ask him."

"Excuse me?"

"Yes?"

"Your husband is dead."

"Oh, yes. But I'll hear from him shortly. I know Jack."

Lucy turned and stared at me. She shook

her head. I grinned. She turned back and bid good-bye to Mrs. Carbondale.

Thankfully, it was easier going down those stairs than coming up. But just as she reached the exit door, Lucy, who was in the lead as usual, stopped short and caused an embarrassing chain reaction of bumps and stumbles among the rest of us. I actually ended up in Peter Marin's arms.

When we had sorted ourselves out, John Wu demanded an explanation.

Lucy pointed to the door, where someone had tried inexpertly to remove a patch of graffiti. Part of the message was still visible.

"Can anyone make out what was written there?" Lucy asked.

We tried, but none of us was able to read it.

"I don't know what it says. What does it matter?" Willa asked.

"Peter, you're a master of illusion," Lucy said. "Do something."

Obviously insulted, he retorted, "What do you mean by that?"

"Only that you're a very successful commercial artist. You know how to play with disappearances and reappearances."

Whew! Sometimes Lucy is quite mystical.

"And you want me to retrieve that message—make it 'reappear,' as you put it. Is that what you're asking me to do?"

"Yes, Peter."

"Well . . ." He looked around. "I suppose I might . . . Willa, do you have any loose face powder?"

She opened her handbag and obliged him.

Peter took the black enamel box, opened it, and blew some powder at the spot on the door where the writing had once been.

He waited for about thirty seconds, then blew much harder on the door itself. Much of the powder floated off. But the lines of what had been written there were now visible.

"Oh, my!" Lucy exclaimed.

We could all see what had been scrawled on the door: "NO REMORSE."

"You see!" a triumphant John Wu crowed. "You were all wrong, Lucy. That was what Carbondale wrote on the wall of his hotel room. And he wrote it here on the door of his studio before he went to the hotel. So the suicide was premeditated. He did plan to kill himself, and he wanted everyone to know that he had no qualms about taking his own life."

There was silence in the hallway.

Finally Lucy said, to no one in particular, "I guess you could say our trip downtown has been a failure."

"At least," Willa Wayne noted, "we now know for a fact that Houston Street is not a bird migration flyway."

We all walked outside. Peter, John, and Willa took a cab uptown. I stood on the sidewalk with Lucy. A truck was unloading huge tin ventilation hoods for restaurant kitchens.

"Suddenly, Markus," she said, "I need sustenance."

"Do you mean food?"

"Precisely."

I offered my arm. She took it.

A short time later we were sitting in a booth in a Chinese coffee shop on Grand Street. We were the only non-Chinese in the place. Lucy stared at the plate of tiny buns, but she didn't eat. And she hadn't touched her coffee.

"I thought you were hungry."

"I was, Markus, but now I'm not. How long did it take us to walk here?"

"About ten minutes."

"Well, that's a long time, Markus, isn't it? A lot can happen in ten minutes. Entire battles are lost in that space of time. Surely a woman like myself, getting on in years, can change from being hungry to not being hungry in ten minutes . . . can't I?"

"Of course you can, Lucy."

"I'm glad you agree."

I intuited that the visit to Carbondale's studio had been disastrous for her, intellectually, that is. So I minded what I said.

"You know, Lucy, sedatives often make rational people act very strangely indeed."

"What do you mean by that?"

"Only that Bo Carbondale, if she hadn't been on medication, would not have made the kind of comments she made to you. I doubt that she really believes her dead husband is about to contact her."

"On the contrary, Markus."

"Contrary?"

"Yes. I think she believes she will be contacted by the departed."

"But how?"

"How should I know! Maybe she expects a raven to fly through the window, perch on a drawing board, and discourse with her."

Before I could digest all that, she changed the subject abruptly.

"So how is Duke faring?" she asked innocuously.

"Who?"

"Your dog, Markus, your dog. Don't you know your own dog's name?"

"Oh, yes, Duke. He's fine. But he sometimes keeps me awake at night."

"How so? He has his own bedroom."

"Thumping."

"Thumping?"

"That's right. Because he has only three legs, sometimes, at night, when he decides to chew on one leg, one of the other legs thumps the floor. I guess it's because he's . . . I guess you could call him . . . unbalanced."

"A small price to pay for such a fine companion. I think it was the best thing I ever did, giving you that dog."

"I am grateful to you, Lucy. In retrospect. But, to be honest, I wouldn't say there is a strong emotional bond between the two of us."

"That's not the dog's fault. Pit bulls can be quite loving. It might be your problem."

"I have no problem loving," I whispered passionately, grabbing her hand across the table.

"Calm yourself, Markus. We're in a strange neighborhood."

I released her hand, chastened, sheepish. If she wanted to make small talk, I would.

"And how is your aunt Hattie?" I asked.

It so happened that Aunt Hattie, Lucy's "down-home" relative, had by chance saved my life during her first visit to New York. I was eternally grateful to the old woman for that, but she persisted in thinking that I was out to corrupt her niece. She just didn't like me at all. *And* she called me Marco, and believed, all evidence to the contrary, that I was a member of the Cosa Nostra.

"I spoke to Aunt Hattie a few days ago," Lucy said. "She's fine. She sends her best to you."

Then she proceeded, in a meticulous manner, to bisect a sweet bun with her fork. She stared at her surgically altered repast but still did not partake of it.

On the wall behind her was a lovely Chinese flower painting.

Lucy sat back and placed both her hands palm down on the table.

"What do you think of that phrase, Markus?"

"What phrase?"

" 'No remorse.' "

"Oh, I don't know. It reminds me of that Edith Piaf song. You know, *'Je ne regrette rien.'* "

"Remorse is not regret," she replied.

"How true."

"But you have seen that term before."

"Yes. Often."

"Where? In what context?"

"I don't remember."

She replied angrily, "But you just said you saw it often. Surely you can remember one instance."

"Okay. Okay. Yes. I can. Do you recall the upheavals in France—in 1968?"

"Vaguely."

"With everyone rioting and the government about to collapse. With the students running through the streets and chalking graffiti everywhere."

"Go on, Markus."

"Well, one of their most popular slogans was No Remorse."

"No remorse for what?"

"I haven't the slightest idea."

She picked up her fork and cut another bun into quarters. "Tell me, Markus," she said quietly, "after all you have heard from me the last few days concerning the death of Jack Wesley Carbondale, and all you saw and heard this morning—do you believe he was murdered?"

I didn't reply.

"It's a simple question," she pressed. "Do you think he jumped or not?"

I didn't answer.

"Why can't you be honest with me, Markus?"

Honest? What the hell does honesty have to do with courtship? Was Cyrano honest?

I replied with, "All I can say, Lucy, is that from this retired physician's viewpoint you are becoming a bit obsessive in this matter."

She leaned across the table and pierced me with a look. "Why shouldn't I be obsessive?" she asked, her voice stern. "Don't we both belong to a worldwide community of birders? And wasn't Carbondale one of our saints?"

This was beyond me.

Chapter 4

We assembled the next morning, all of us, same time, same place.

Lucy's speculations and the debacle of the studio visit seemed to have been forgotten.

But there was plenty of avian electricity.

John Wu knew an economics professor who knew a union negotiator who knew a Parks Department contractor who said there was a bufflehead duck in the pond near Central Park South.

Peter Marin did him one better. A doorman he knew had told him that a jogger had seen greater scaups in the reservoir, interspersed with the lesser scaups.

And Willa, to everyone's surprise, said that she had learned from an unnamed but trustworthy source that there were still yellow-rumped warblers in the Upper Lobe.

It was a bonanza of classified information—all, some, or none of which might be true. Birders live on rumors. That is half the fun—tracking the tips down and validating the tipsters, informers, and casual spies.

We stood in front of the statue and waited for our leader to evaluate the intelligence and lead us onto the field of battle.

Lucy Wayles stared across the park entrance at the spire of the Church of the Heavenly Dove. She was thinking it through. I could tell that. Her head was slightly cocked. She kept shifting the knapsack on her back ever so slightly, almost imperceptibly.

The troops kept closing the circle about her—toes squeaking in their hiking boots, sweating fingers tightening around binocular straps in the chilly autumn morning.

Even I was getting somewhat excited.

"The yellow-rumped warblers," Lucy told us, "are always the last to leave in the fall. I think we are obligated to say good-bye to them. I think we should let them know we appreciate their tenacity."

There was no resistance. Off we went.

We found the warblers quickly. They were in trees on the far slope of the Upper Lobe, which is merely a fancy name for a small, watery spur separated from the main Central Park lake by a sand spur.

These warblers were old friends. We knew all their feeding moves.

But the vegetation was very sparse now, so they gave us one of those unexpected bird-watching thrills.

They started to skim over the water, hunting insects. They moved slowly, then fast, in delirious, unpredictable patterns.

"Like swallows!" a startled but happy Lucy gushed.

When the feeding frenzy was over and the hardy warblers reoccupied the tree limbs, we moved off to find the bufflehead duck.

We never got there. The wind stirred up, the heavens opened, and we ended our expedition sipping hot chocolate in the zoo cafeteria.

It wasn't one of our better outings, but fall and winter bird-watching is always chancy. Anyway, it turned out well for me because Lucy invited me to her apartment after Olmsted's Irregulars disbanded for the day.

I interpreted this to mean that our courtship was back on track.

Oh, it was wonderful being in Lucy's small,

sun-drenched apartment on 93rd Street just east of Fifth Avenue again. The clutter had gotten worse, though. Stacks of books, magazines, clipped articles, and objects that no longer fit on the shelves or in bookcases littered the floor.

I did, however, feel a bit uneasy. Where was Dipper? Where was Lucy's cat?

Lucy had found Dipper a few years ago on a trip to Hawk Mountain. He was on the roof of a convenience store. The big cat liked only high places, so Lucy named him after the Big Dipper. In Lucy's apartment he draped himself over bookcases, shower curtains, kitchen cabinets. Anyplace but on the floor.

Dipper didn't like me. That was why I had to know where he was at all times. He always gave me evil looks from on high, and I constantly felt he was a second away from pouncing. Of course, Lucy said I was fantasizing; she swore that Dipper adored me.

Well, that afternoon I simply couldn't locate the beast.

Lucy made coffee and we sat in front of her large windows in separate easy chairs.

"Where's Dipper?" I asked finally.

"About. Why?"

"Just curious. I didn't see him when I came in."

"Look closer, Markus, and you'll find him."

"Probably."

"I've mentioned this on several occasions to you."

"Mentioned what?"

"That you never look closely enough at things. And when you *do* look closely enough, you don't look *long* enough."

"I think you misjudge me, Lucy."

"No. No. It is astonishing to me that here you are . . . a trained scientist who conducted sophisticated experiments into the cold virus in the laboratory. But once out of your lab you tend to . . . ah, Markus . . . let me be honest . . . you tend to be a bit of a bumbler."

"A bumbler?" I wasn't hurt. Just confused.

"Well, let us go on to more serious topics," she said.

"Fine," I agreed.

"What have you been reading, Markus?"

"A book on Cuba."

"A novel?"

"No. A political history from the 1840s to the present."

"Why are you reading about Cuba?"

"I don't know. I just am. Actually my heart isn't in it, Lucy."

"What do you mean?"

"I really want to read about Uruguay."

She was silent. I heard a movement on the far side of the room, high up. Was it Dipper? Was he stalking me?

"Did you hear me, Lucy?"

"Yes. You mentioned something about Uruguay."

"It is the funniest thing. I have suddenly, out of the blue, developed a passion for that country. Believe me. I don't know where it is in South America. I don't know anyone from Uruguay. I don't know what language they speak, what food they eat, what clothes they wear. I don't even know the capital of Uruguay, Lucy."

She was staring intently out the window.

"Did you ever have such a strange, quirky passion suddenly erupt, Lucy?"

"Yes."

"What was it?"

"It would be best if that were left unsaid."

"Well, I don't wish to pry, Lucy, dear."

"You know, Markus Bloch, that is a word you seem to be using excessively these days."

"What word?"

"Passion."

"I wasn't aware of that."

"There's nothing wrong with using it, of course, but you tend to use it the wrong way."

"How so?"

"One really doesn't develop 'passion' for Uruguay—or Canada, for that matter. For strawberries, perhaps. But not for countries."

"But, Lucy, it's a common enough expression. I hear people say things like 'I have a passion for France' every day in the week."

"Markus. You are confusing usage with propriety. And that is a fool's game."

The sun was dipping in and out of the clouds, sending all kinds of weird shadows up and down 93rd Street and into Lucy's apartment. I luxuriated in our small conversations, our small disagreements. This was the kind of domesticity I craved . . . with her.

"Aren't your nephew's children due for a visit?" Lucy asked.

"In about two weeks, I think."

"How old are they now?"

"Nine and eleven."

"What will you do with them?"

"I don't know. But I think they like hockey."

Lucy closed her eyes and seemed to be taking a slight, happy nap. But then she opened her eyes, blinked, sat up and back, and asked, "What about the Hilton, Markus?"

"For those children? Don't be ridiculous, Lucy. I have a three-bedroom apartment. And only two are currently being lived in."

"I meant for us," Lucy said quietly.

I was too shocked to say anything.

"I meant," Lucy added urgently, *"for tonight."*

Whoa!

My God! This was what I had been waiting for. This was the final step. Yes! A night of love with Lucy Wayles. She had forgiven and forgotten my past sexual failing. Soon there would be the final beautiful act of consummation . . . and then there would be marriage and blessed companionship . . . and Lucy and I, hand in hand, circling the globe looking for rarer and rarer birds.

I was deep in a dream.

"Did you hear what I said, Markus?"

I still couldn't speak but I started to pump my head vigorously.

"Good. Now, I want you to check in alone."

My heart sank.

"Why alone?" I fairly shouted, and then heard a terrible noise and saw that Dipper was on top of the main bookcase glaring at me and the crash was a book on ancient Greek pottery that he had sent plummeting to the floor.

"I will be there later on in the evening, Markus."

I broke into a huge, lascivious but basically tender grin. Now I understood. It was to be an all-out tryst. Two lovers meeting in secret. Oh, Lucy was unbelievable. Astonishing. She was . . .

"Markus, there is one other thing you should know before you start moving."

I was already halfway to the door. I had showers to take, a dog to walk, a reservation to make, champagne to order. "Yes, Lucy dear?"

"I want you to take room 1502."

"What did you say?"

"Get room 1502."

"But, Lucy, isn't . . . wasn't that Carbondale's room?"

"I believe it was."

I looked at her. I couldn't imagine what this new development meant.

"Meeting in the room where he—well, isn't it kind of morbid?"

"Humor me, dear Markus."

At that moment I would have rented that tower in London where the two young boys were murdered.

"Of course I'll get room 1502," I affirmed. And then added the most ridiculous rationale: "After all, he didn't jump *into* the room, did he? He jumped out of it."

I rushed out, waving to the menacing Dipper as I ran.

Chapter 5

Because time was of the essence that afternoon, I made several key errors. Most important, I should not have alienated Duke. But I was in such a hurry. So I didn't take him to the park as usual on his afternoon walk; we just went around the block and then west.

He got angry. He decided not to move. He stopped. He sat down. I pleaded. I begged. I threatened to leave him there on the street and let some stranger deal with him.

Of course, all I had to do was pick up the three-legged monster and carry him home. Duke weighed only about forty pounds.

But I am afraid of pit bulls. Duke really hadn't exhibited any of the violence of his breed yet—but I could tell he was on the cusp. Anyway, in order to get him walking again and home again, so that I could proceed with important matters, I had to resort to the most blatant and embarrassing kind of bribery: purchasing tidbits of meat in a local butcher shop and luring him back home inch by inch. Finally, with Duke in his room, I called for the hotel reservation. But I knew that eventually the Duke problem would come back to haunt me. I mean, when Lucy moved in with me, which could happen sooner or later, she would bring Dipper. So—what to do with Duke? It was doubtful that they could coexist. Even if they could, it would be worrisome. Remember, it was Lucy who brought Duke into my life; who rescued him from the kennel. In addition to being a pit bull, Duke is very much a gangster dog. He had belonged to a notorious drug dealer. He was wounded in the DEA raid that killed his master. He probably had underworld proclivities of the worst kind.

All these Duke-related problems would have to be resolved. Actually, the idea of staying in my apartment with a menace on the floor and a menace above was not palatable to me, even with Lucy. That kind of constant nerve-wracking threat just didn't make sense in a home with two mature lovebirds, if you'll pardon the mawkish expression.

Just as I picked up the phone to call the Hilton, that funny word "Uruguay" popped into my head again. I slammed the phone down to conduct a simple therapy and get that mysterious country out of my head. I repeated the word out loud five times, ten times, a hundred times, until it sickened me. Then I had a tiny bit of brandy and dialed the hotel.

All went well at the beginning.

Yes, they had a room available. The rate was $225 per night for a double.

With a choice of double bed or twin beds. I opted for the former.

"How long will you be staying?" the reservations clerk asked.

"I'm not sure. At least two nights."

"Cash or charge?"

"Cash."

"A phone number where you can be reached."

I gave him two, my own and Lucy's.

"What time will you be arriving?"

"I'll check in around six. Mrs. Bloch won't be arriving until later."

Saying those words—Mrs. Bloch—gave me a palpitation.

Then the trouble started.

"One more thing," I told the clerk. "I would like to have room 1502."

There was silence on the other end of the line.

"Are you still there?"

"I'm afraid room 1502 isn't available, Mr. Bloch. It's being refurbished."

"Look, I know that a tragedy occurred there recently. And I know that when such things happen hotels tend to withdraw the room from circulation, so to speak, because it attracts oddballs who like to sleep in such places—at the scene of a terrible event. It's a kind of sick, retroactive voyeurism. But believe me, we're not that type of people. And I happen to know that the room was not damaged. One wall was defaced with a crayon or magic marker or some such. At most, you gave it a quick paint job. Please—I know it's habitable and that's the room I want."

Again, the deadly silence. And then the infuriating repetition of the litany of reasons. "What we can do," the clerk added this time, "is give you another room on the same floor—the fifteenth floor."

"No! It must be 1502."

"I'm sorry."

Suddenly that word was back in my mind: "Uruguay." Along with the word "Borges." And then the word "Argentina." The human mind as it ages is a marvelous garbage pail of images and words. I realized I had remembered the country Uruguay from a story I'd read many years ago by the writer Borges about a gaucho who murdered a man in Argentina and fled to Uruguay.

For some reason, the recovery of that memory sequence enabled me to construct an elaborate lie and recite it to the reservations clerk.

"Listen, my friend. I used to be coordinator of CBS News foreign bureaus. Fifteen years ago I met a young Argentine journalist named Luca Walo. We fell in love and we married in a week. We honeymooned in room 1502 of your hotel. Then she went back home. She was picked up by an army death squad. She became one of the hundred thousand or so 'disappeared ones.' But it turned out she was five years in jail and ten years in a mental hospital. Ten days ago, after fifteen long years, I spoke to my wife again. She is arriving from Buenos Aires tonight. I have to have that room. Do you understand?"

There was a very long pause. "Please hold the line," a scratchy voice said at last.

He came back on the line after five excruciating minutes.

"Yes, all right," he said. "We'll be expecting you, Mr. Bloch. And there will be some flowers for Mrs. Bloch—from the management."

I must admit, I was proud of myself. When I do lie, I do it right.

So there I was, at 6:00 P.M., ensconced in room 1502.

The room was quite lovely. There was a long hallway with a bathroom on the left. On the right was one of those small convenience rooms with only a sink and a refrigerator, and next to it, a huge closet. Then the main room with the windows looking north; a jumbo bed with tables on either side; a writing table, a sofa, two chairs, a big color television atop a swiveling table, and a floral arrangement from the manager welcoming my long-suffering, long-lost Argentinean wife.

Yes, all was ready. I figured Lucy would arrive around nine. At eight o'clock I called room service and two waiters brought up a cold repast along with our champagne. They left the elegantly laden cart in front of the writing table.

Then I lay down on the sumptuous bed and surveyed my domain.

Perfect. Perfect. Perfect. Everything in its place.

Not everything! I jumped up and bustled over to the window. I had to draw the curtains. If Lucy came in and saw the windows first—the windows looking north on 54th Street—she would immediately think of Carbondale leaping, and that would distract her.

So I pulled at the curtains until there was only a sliver of glass pane visible if one looked hard.

The knock came at around twenty minutes to nine.

I sauntered to the door and opened it with a flourish.

Lucy Wayles stepped inside, lovelier than ever. She was wearing that strange black dress she had worn to Abraham Lescalles' memorial service last year. And she was wearing a new floppy hat . . . looking every inch the wild, aging flapper she was. My head began to spin.

"How are you, Markus?" she asked sweetly.

I grabbed her and pulled her to me.

Whap!

She hit me on top of the head with the heel of her hand.

I staggered backward.

"What are you doing, Markus!"

"Just trying to hold you, my dear."

She walked to the chair and sat down primly, removing her hat. "I don't have time for that kind of nonsense."

Nonsense? The whole fantasy of a night of intimacy with my true love was crumbling swiftly.

"I am here to conduct a search, Markus. And I expect you to provide clearheaded assistance."

"What?"

"You heard me, Markus. A search. Why do you think I asked you to rent this room?"

The last piece of the last hope dribbled away.

"What are we searching for?" I asked, defeated.

"Information pertaining to the premeditated murder of Jack Wesley Carbondale."

"The police, I am sure, have already searched this room thoroughly."

"How do you know that, Markus?"

"Because that is what police do."

"I think you are mistaken. I think the only thing they searched for was a suicide note, which they did not find."

"What are we looking for if not a suicide note?"

She didn't answer. She scanned the walls, looking, I assume, for the one on which had been scrawled NO REMORSE. But the room had been painted over; that was sure. And there was no sign of the graffiti.

"I feel, Markus, like a woodpecker who stashed some gourmet acorns and now can't locate them."

"Shall I tell you what I feel like, Lucy? I feel confused."

"Sit down, Markus."

I sat down on the side of the bed.

"Now listen to me. It is quite simple. I believe that Carbondale hid something in this room."

"Why hide something just before committing suicide?"

"Forget suicide!"

"I thought you were cured of your brief obsession."

"There is no such thing as a brief obsession. A physician should know that. Here is what I think: Carbondale was waiting for someone. The murderer. Carbondale might or might not have had suspicions concerning his visitor. Either way, he hid something. Because, dear Markus, this was not an ordinary visit. Oh, no. It was too close to the awards ceremony. This was some kind of crucial meeting."

"Lucy, this is all the wildest kind of speculation."

"Speculation, yes. Wild, no. Don't you feel it, Markus?"

"Feel what?"

She leaned over. "That somewhere in this room is the answer. Oh, it's here. We're like owls sitting high on the barn rafters, in the dark, our great flat owl faces absorbing the sound waves like a sonar screen. We hear the tiniest rustle. Ever so soft . . . and then . . ." She stood suddenly. "And then we leave the rafter and hone in on our meal."

She sat down again, exhausted.

"Would you like a cracker with some pâté?" I offered.

She regarded me as if I were crazy.

"Or some champagne?"

Then she adjusted. "I suppose it couldn't hurt. Why not fuel up before the search?" she said.

So we ate a bit and drank a bit from the room service tray.

"Tell me, Markus," Lucy said contentedly after our repast, "where would you hide something in this room?—if you were Jack Carbondale, that is."

"I haven't the slightest idea."

"Nor do I, and that is the problem. I guess we will simply have to conduct an old-fashioned search. Like crazy Uncle Wyatt had died and you know he left twenty gold coins somewhere in his cabin."

"Twenty gold coins are twenty gold coins! We don't even know what we're looking for," I noted.

Lucy did not find the comment relevant. We began the search. And believe me, it was thorough. We felt beneath the carpet. We removed every drawer. We went through the bathroom and the dressing room like vacuums. We moved the small refrigerator and upended the mattress. We unscrewed light bulbs. We turned the writing table over and unscrewed its legs.

We ravaged the few pictures on the walls and the elegant paper cup dispensers.

At ten o'clock we collapsed, Lucy on the chair and I on the bed.

"Would you like more champagne?" I asked.

"No."

"Maybe if you had told me what this adventure was all about before I rented the room, Lucy, I would have come better prepared for the search."

"Prepared how?"

"I could have brought Duke along. He would have sniffed out the drugs."

My joke went flat. In fact, it irritated Lucy.

She turned on me angrily. "Why are the curtains drawn, Markus? Was that your idea?"

She jumped out of her chair, strode to the window, and ripped the curtains apart.

Then she let out a yelp that made me jump six inches in the air.

"What is it?"

Lucy began to hop. "That stupid curtain smashed into my ankle!" she explained.

"How could a curtain 'smash' into anything?"

The profundity of my question was immediately apparent.

We both ran, in our fashion, back to the window.

Yes, the bottom hem of one side of the curtain was weighted. It was as if someone had opened the hem and slid part of a curtain rod inside.

Carefully, Lucy sat down on the rug next to the window and pushed the object out. I sat beside her.

She held the object up.

"It looks like a screwdriver," I said. "At least from the handle."

And only the handle was visible. A white sheet of paper was wrapped tightly around the rest of the tool and secured by some kind of elastic band.

Lucy pulled the elastic band off. Then the paper.

No, it wasn't a screwdriver. It was an old-fashioned, wicked-looking ice pick.

Next Lucy examined the elastic band. "It's a garter," she announced.

The object touched off a dim memory. I hadn't seen one of those in an age. "I do believe you're right," I said.

Then she unfurled what turned out to be a piece of eight-by-fourteen-inch drawing paper.

On it was an astonishing sight: a large bird drawn in heavy black ink, filling most of the page. But it was not a regular bird drawing. Even I knew that. It was an antiquated genre—a bird silhouette with wings spread.

This was the kind of illustration found in very old field and hunting guides, included so that an identification could be made on shape alone. The same method had been used by the U.S. Navy during World War II to train gunners to spot the difference between their own fighters and the aircraft of the enemy.

"I need more light," Lucy said. She gathered all the objects carefully and carried them to the bed.

She looked at them a long time. Then she said, "Tell me, Markus. In the first place, why would Jack Carbondale hide a bird drawing? And second, why would he wrap it around an ice pick? And why use a woman's garter instead of a plain old rubber band?"

"I have no idea."

She handed the drawing to me. "Look at the wings," she ordered.

I did so.

"Are they familiar to you, Markus?"

"No," I replied honestly.

"They should be, Dr. Bloch. They're the wings of a falcon."

"Yes, Lucy, now I see. I think you're right."

"And the head?"

"Well . . . I . . . I'm not sure."

"Much like a skua's."

"Oh, of course, dear."

"And the feet, Markus?"

I nodded. "Very familiar indeed."

"Yes. The feet are those of a diving duck."

"Right again."

"So what type of bird are we looking at?" she asked.

"I'm . . . ah . . . unsure."

"You should be unsure. Because there *is* no bird with a falcon's wings, a skua's head, and a diving duck's feet."

"Then why did he draw it that way?"

"How do we know Carbondale drew it?" she countered.

"Oh, of course. We don't."

"What do we know, Markus?"

"Not much."

Lucy placed her hand affectionately on my cheek. "There's one very important thing we know," she said.

"What?"

"That you and I have taken one giant step toward apprehending the person or persons who murdered Jack Wesley Carbondale."

Chapter 6

It was a very unusual meeting of Olmsted's Irregulars.

We always meet in the park, but this meeting took place in my apartment.

We always meet on weekdays, never weekends—we leave the park to the tourists then. But this meeting was held on Sunday afternoon, three o'clock in the afternoon, to be precise.

When we were assembled and comfortably seated, a very officious-looking Lucy removed the objects we had found in the hotel and laid them carefully on the low coffee table.

She addressed us gravely. "Will you all please file by and look at the exhibits."

John Wu stood first and headed for the table. While he was peering down at the ob-

jects and Willa and Peter were lining up behind him, we all heard the clip-clopping of
Duke's progress as he hopped and hobbled
into the room. The dog stopped in his tracks
and evaluated the assembled.

Lucy and I exchanged nervous looks: Duke
had a very queer expression on his face. He
looked like a shy suitor arriving for a blind
date. And while I didn't know much about pit
bulls, I did know that one of the reasons they
are disliked so much is that they don't show
the usual signals of aggression before attack-
ing. They exhibit what is called paradoxical
rage. In other words, you think you're going
to get your face licked and instead you find
your wrist in a vise.

As Duke stood there, his ugly mug became
positively beatific. Oh, yes, there was a clear
and present danger. As usual, I didn't know
what to do.

Lucy, however, did. She let loose a whoop of
joy and cried out in a broad Southern, almost
vaudevillian drawl: "Oh my! It's mah lovely
Doggie! Aren't you pretty!"

Then she rushed him, swooped all forty
pounds of the three-legged time bomb into her

arms, and began to rock him like a fretful baby.

She called out to the group as though she were a tour guide in a museum: "Will you please continue to observe the exhibit. We're on a schedule."

The Irregulars obeyed her. Lucy carried Duke back to his room, reasoned with him for a while, and then shut the bedroom door and returned to the living room.

We were all seated again. Lucy glared at us. "I need your help, people. These strange objects were found in Mr. Carbondale's hotel room. He hid them before he was murdered."

When she enunciated the word "murdered," a long, low groan of exasperation escaped Peter's throat. He knew, as we all did now, that Lucy had not let go of her obsession.

Lucy walked briskly to the coffee table, picked up the bird silhouette, held it against her chest like a kindergarten teacher showing a picture of a sweet little cow to the children.

"Above all," she said, "I need your help with this bird. Can any of you identify it?"

There was silence.

Then she walked the drawing around the room three times, each time shoving it into the field of vision of one of the Irregulars. (I was made to suffer it only twice. I guess she was giving me credit for the time I had put in at the Hilton.)

She returned to the coffee table, laid the drawing back down, turned, and demanded, "What say you?"

Willa picked a tiny fleck of apartment dust off her lovely shoulder and said, "It won't do any good to show me that thing again, Lucy. I've really never seen a bird like it. Not even in a book."

"It's nonsense," John said impatiently. "Maybe Carbondale was under the influence when he drew it."

Peter Marin, ever the commercial artist, added, "It's probably a pasteup of some kind."

"So what? What does that mean?" John demanded.

"He took the head from some bird that really exists, the beak of another, a foot from another, and so on and so on," answered Peter.

"Peter must be right," I offered.

Lucy looked at us. There was an uncommon sense of desperation about her. "Is that all you can say?" she demanded. Her words were met with a collective shrug.

She whirled, picked up the garter. "What are your thoughts about this?"

We had none.

Then she held up the ice pick.

John spoke up before she had a chance to ask another question. "You can't even buy those things anymore. The ice pick has gone the way of the buggy whip. No one sells block ice anymore."

Peter added smugly, "You know, Lucy, just because you found this strange assortment of objects in Carbondale's room doesn't mean they have anything to do with him. They could have been put in that curtain by a previous guest a week before Jack Carbondale checked in at the hotel . . . a month before . . . a year before."

Miss Wayles didn't like that at all. She turned to me stonily. "Markus, isn't it time you served your guests some refreshments?"

"But I have nothing in the house."

"Then go down and get some coffee and tea and some sort of tidbits to go along with them."

"Yes, Lucy."

I left hurriedly and gathered the provisions.

When I returned—it couldn't have been

more than fifteen minutes later—everyone was gone except Lucy.

"Where is everyone?"

"They've left. The meeting was adjourned," she said crisply.

"But what about the coffee and tea?"

"Use it to clean your rug, Markus. It surely could use some looking after."

I sat down heavily, confused again.

"During an investigation, Markus, when time is of the essence, one has to be ruthless."

"You mean you kicked them all out?"

"Don't be crude. Of course not. But, as you saw and heard for yourself, our comrades were of little help. And we have roads to travel, Markus."

"Roads? What roads?"

"As soon as you recover, we are going back down to the Bowery."

"To Carbondale's studio, you mean?"

"Yes, that's right."

"But it's Sunday."

"So?"

"But you saw the shape his widow was in. She can't be of any help to you . . . us."

"We're not going there to talk to Bo Carbondale. It's those three assistants that we want to speak with. And we shall."

There is no arguing with Lucy Wayles when she uses that emphatic "shall."

It was the researcher, Don Franco, who opened the door to the Bowery studio.

"Yes?" he asked. A sweatband held his long silvery hair in place. Given the fact that he had to be past fifty, it looked ridiculous. Not to Lucy, of course, since she herself wore a band very much like it whenever she went birding.

Franco obviously did not remember us. Lucy refreshed his memory.

"Oh, right. Now I remember. I'm sorry. It's been hectic here. But you missed Bo by about an hour."

"Actually, I've come to see you," Lucy said.

"Oh? What about?"

She stepped past him and into the studio, pulling me after her.

"Did you find the gull plates yet, Mr. Franco? Or the stats?"

He gave us an arch look, as if questioning why the whereabouts of the artwork should be any of our business.

But then he did answer. "No, not yet. But

we will. Jack was a secretive kind of person. He kept everything close to the vest. That was fine when he was alive."

He went back to a carton he had been rummaging through, in the center of the loft. It was clear he was not happy with our visit. We watched him root through the contents of the box. He was in quite good shape, trim, light on his feet. And he was emptying the carton with authority and rapidity, pulling out an assortment of pads, old paint tubes, and all kinds of weird objects.

It was just as obvious that he had been instructed to search every possible nook and cranny for the missing gulls.

"What does a researcher do?" Lucy asked him.

Without breaking his rhythm he replied nastily, "Research."

Lucy was undaunted. "I meant, research in what area?"

"What the hell do you imagine?" Franco snapped.

But immediately afterward, he calmed himself and stopped his search. He made eye contact with Lucy and answered evenly, showing respect, even if it was mixed with a little condescension. "I collect and collate all new bird guides being published all over the world. I clip newspaper articles about bird sightings. I read and send for reprints of important papers published in scholarly journals like the *Auk*. That is the kind of work I do. And all kinds of other tasks—some of them not so intelligent."

I found the brief description of his work quite interesting. It had really never dawned on me how much work went into preparing a field guide for publication. It isn't a cookbook, after all. There has to be current information on each bird, from migration patterns to nesting habits to its parasites. No wonder Carbondale had his own staff.

Franco was now waiting for us to leave. He had obviously answered all the questions he was going to answer.

Or so he thought. Lucy thought otherwise.

She moved close to him, sort of circling to his left.

The researcher kept his eyes on the both of us. I had the distinct impression that he thought I might steal something or other as a memento.

"Were you aware that Carbondale was murdered?" Lucy asked him directly.

"Excuse me—what did you say?" the startled Franco replied.

"You heard me correctly, young man. I asked you if you were aware of the fact that Jack Carbondale was thrown from that fifteenth-floor window."

"That's what I thought you said. I just couldn't believe it at first. That's the stupidest thing I ever—" He broke off there, his temper rising. "What are you trying to do, Miss Wayles? Fabricate a story and sell it to the *Enquirer* so you can fly down to Belize and finally add a monkey-eating eagle or some other prize rare bird to your life list? Is that it—you want to cash in on Jack's death? Or are you just a garden-variety New York nut?"

"Really, Mr. Franco," Lucy said, untroubled by his aggression, "I don't think your associates would treat this information so cavalierly."

"Is that so? Well, why don't you go tell them?"

"I hope to. Where are they?"

"In Fanelli's, taking a break . . . Lucky people."

"You are a very unaccommodating man, Mr. Franco."

"Only when people take up my time with nonsense."

"If what I told you is nonsense," Lucy said, "then what do you make of this?"

Lucy unfolded the drawing we'd found in the hem of the hotel curtain.

"What is that?"

"Look for yourself, Mr. Franco." She held it out to him.

Don Franco seemed to be hesitating. He wanted to see what it was, but he didn't want to encourage someone who he clearly believed was deranged.

Finally, after shaking his hand like an athlete trying to stimulate his circulation, he took the paper and studied it. He stared at it for a good long time.

"What is this?" he finally asked, alarm showing in his eyes.

"A bird silhouette drawn by Carbondale and hidden in his hotel room before the murder."

Franco looked down at the drawing again; he looked back up at Lucy; he looked over at me. When he returned the paper to Lucy, he became extremely polite, saying, "May I make three points?"

"By all means!" she said.

"All right. Point one: Jack Carbondale did not do silhouettes.

"Two: This isn't a bird, it's a hallucination.

"And three: If you and your friend do not leave immediately, I will call the police."

"You are no gentleman," Lucy replied quietly. She turned on her heel, nodded to me, and wordlessly led the way out of the loft.

When we reached the street, I took her arm and led her to the curb.

"Where are you dragging me, Markus?"

"To get a cab back uptown."

"No. We're not going uptown."

"Why not?"

"Because we're going to Fanelli's," she said. And then added, "I assume, Markus, that because of your unsavory past you know where that establishment is."

She was making a joke. But I did indeed know exactly where Fanelli's was.

We walked there in a few minutes—west on Prince Street as the crow flies.

And there it stood. It was almost dark when we arrived, but I was amazed at how little the outside of the bar had changed. It had been twenty-five years since I had been in Fanelli's. Back then it was just a neighborhood place for starving artists. That was before SoHo became millionaire's row.

We walked inside. The interior hadn't changed at all—the old high wooden break-front behind the bar was intact. And the crush of bodies hadn't changed either. The bar had been packed the last time I was there, and it was packed now.

"You do remember what they look like, don't you?" Lucy asked me testily.

"A tall Abe Lincoln kind of fellow and a thinly delicate lady with a University of Miami sweatshirt," I replied proudly, even though I was being buffeted as we worked our way deeper inside, between the bar drinkers and the tables that lined the wall opposite the bar.

"The sweatshirt said 'Johns Hopkins,'" Lucy corrected, urging me on from behind.

A waitress loomed in front of me with a tray of food. She glared at me. *What had I done?* She elbowed her way past me, muttering. But no food had fallen.

Lucy started whispering in my ear as she intensified her pushing to get me to move farther and faster. "Remember their names, Markus. The artist is Maurice Drabkin. The writer is Norma Hennion."

"Let's find them first. Then I'll remember."

We didn't find them. They found us. Norma Hennion was waving wildly at us from just inside the crowded dining room at the back. If I remembered correctly, in the old days that was a room set aside for ladies who wished to meet and drink at a remove from what could become a pretty raucous atmosphere in the barroom up front.

"Here! Over here!" she kept calling out.

When we reached the small table, Norma, plainly pie-eyed, began to gush. "Hi, you two! I saw you come in and recognized you immediately. I said to Maurice, 'There're two of those wonderful crazy bird-watchers who came up to pay their respects to Bo the other day.' Didn't I say that, Maury?" She poked her companion, who was slouched in the chair beside her. He nodded morosely.

Miss Hennion dragged over two chairs for us and we joined them at the table.

"Don Franco told us you'd be here," Lucy said.

"Awww," Norma said disappointedly. "And

I thought it was just one of those wonderful coincidences."

"No," Lucy said primly, "not a coincidence. We're here on business." Inebriated people brought out Lucy's severe side.

"Well, madam," Maurice Drabkin said, showing some severity of his own, "state your goddamn business."

"First," Norma pleaded, "have a little something. You must."

Lucy and I ordered small ales. Norma was drinking martinis—and took advantage of the opportunity to order another one, as long as the waitress was there—and Drabkin had whiskey, straight, with a bottle of beer as accompaniment.

Lucy did not wait for our drinks to arrive. She took out a tissue and wiped the top of the table. Then she extracted the bird silhouette from her bag and spread the drawing out.

"Would you kindly look at this," she said.

Drabkin spun the drawing around so that it was directly in front of him, studied it for a moment, and then turned it toward Norma Hennion. She looked at it intently. After all, she was the one who actually wrote the bird guides . . . she annotated each of Jack Wesley Carbondale's drawings.

Then she pushed it away and took a healthy swallow of her martini.

"Well?" asked Lucy. "Has either of you ever seen it before?"

They shook their heads.

"I have reason to believe that Jack Carbondale drew this."

Drabkin guffawed. "You're all wet, lady. I've been working for Jack for years. I do all or most of the preliminary drawings. He never did silhouettes. If that's a Carbondale . . ." He picked up his beer bottle. " . . . then this is a Warhol."

"I also have reason to believe," Lucy continued undaunted, "that Carbondale was murdered. That his leap was forced."

Norma Hennion's laughter threatened to turn hysterical at any moment. "Jack murdered! What a wonderful idea," she was finally able to say. "I should have thought of it myself. The man was a cheap sonofabitch. The only thing he could do was paint birds." She looked to Maurice Drabkin for affirmation and he glumly gave it.

"That sonofabitch made a *lot* of money,"

Norma went on, "and he paid us beans . . . beans!" She began to laugh again. "Lima beans, baked beans, mung beans, green beans. How many damn beans are there in a bean-bag?"

She looked at me flirtatiously. "You are kind of cute," she said. "Dumpy but cute. Like Humpty-Dumpty."

I thanked her for the compliment.

Suddenly Maurice Drabkin's hand shot across the table and fastened around Lucy's wrist like a vise.

At the same time he was looking desperately at Norma Hennion. "Why not tell the truth?" he said, his voice low. "Why hide what we know? What are we frightened of?"

He looked at Lucy again, who was wincing from his hold. "Did you ever hear of Gamma 44?" he asked in a whisper.

"No."

"They're a murderous group, you know. For years they've been making death threats against Carbondale. Both at his home in Connecticut and in the New York studio. They had vowed to kill him because of the 1981 field guide. Do you remember it? It contained that brown pelican watercolor. Two pelicans at a nesting site. The female was bringing nest-building materials to the male and he was constructing it. Gamma 44 demanded that the illo be withdrawn. They gave Carbondale proof that in the pelican world it is the male who gathers and the female who builds. But Jack would not recant. And they vowed retribution."

He suddenly released Lucy's wrist and sighed. "Oh, those violent feminists. Who knew they would carry out their threats?"

Lucy closed her eyes. When she opened them, she said, "Marcus, I do believe we are being made fun of."

She stood up and headed for the exit. I followed. We passed our ales, on their way to the table.

Once outside, she pressed her face against my shoulder. "I am growing weary," she said.

"Yes, dear."

Chapter 7

So, once again, Lucy Wayles, encountering one stone wall after another, ended her investigation into the death of America's premier bird artist.

Or, so it seemed.

About ten days before Thanksgiving every member of Olmsted's Irregulars received a note from Bo Carbondale—the exact same note. In it, she thanked each of us for our condolence visit and invited each of us to a reception being held at a posh 57th Street gallery for the belated opening of her new artwork.

Only Lucy and Peter Marin showed any eagerness to attend. Of course, once Lucy made her choice, I adjusted mine.

Lucy, Peter, and I arrived at the second-floor gallery a little after six o'clock. The opening was one of those "after work" affairs, from six to eight.

Only nine Bo Carbondale's were hung. They occupied a single room. What kind of artist was she? Well, it's hard to describe. She painted landscapes in a rather surreal manner. The subjects were always flat—deserts, plains, pampas, veldts. And the colors were extremely pale.

To be honest, I didn't like them at all, and in fact I made a joke about them to Lucy. "Maybe she killed her husband because he told her what he thought about her paintings," I quipped.

Peter thought my remark was in bad taste. So did Lucy. I promptly shut up.

The space was becoming crowded with wine-sipping guests. We finished viewing the paintings and headed toward the drinks and snacks table. It was a serve-yourself affair. Along with the wine and designer water and tidbits were postcards announcing the show and giving a brief bio of the artist.

"I don't see any of the studio assistants," I said.

Lucy looked around. She nodded in agreement.

"I don't even see Mrs. Carbondale," I added.

"Then who is that?" Peter inquired.

Indeed, Bo was coming directly at us, smiling robustly. If she was heavily medicated the first time we'd met her, she was now on some kind of prescription Boeing 727 upper. Her eyes looked like a cat's eyes at dusk.

She grasped each of our hands in turn and pumped vigorously, saying, "I can't tell you how happy I am that you came. After all, you are Jack's people."

Then she just stood by us and surveyed the people in the room, a slaphappy grin on her face. It was a mixed bag of visitors. Old and young. Scruffy and fashionable. Uptown and downtown. We seemed, however, to be the only bird-watchers.

For some reason, the milieu made me frisky. "Have you made contact yet?" I asked Bo Carbondale.

Peter and Lucy threw visual daggers at me. But it was too late.

Bo Carbondale sidled close to me, grabbed

my arm, and asked in a passionate voice: "Do you mean with Jack?"

I nodded.

"Oh," she said confidingly, "it is a treacherous and frustrating thing, this fraternity of the dead and the living. So many souls intersecting. But not yet . . . not yet. There are hints, though! There are preliminary advances. There are tiny openings. A salt shaker is moved, and I know there was no one who could have moved it. A song comes out of the air and into my head and I know all the words—but I've never heard the song before. So many little things, but—"

Then she just wandered off. "I think," Lucy announced, "we should take one last crack at the paintings and then exit."

"Exactly what I was thinking," Peter said.

We started off quickly, but Lucy slowed down when we approached the painting labeled as number 3, a particularly strange one that depicted some kind of salt flat.

Two people in front of the painting were engaged in a heated discussion. Lucy, obviously, enjoyed eavesdropping at galleries. I did as well. But Peter walked on.

The woman was wearing an outlandish

hat, a kind of baseball cap with earflaps. The man was dressed in a stylish light green suit with a striped polo shirt.

She said: "We're skirting the issue. We're talking art magazine drivel. Obscure."

He said, a bit angrily, staring hard at the canvas: "Okay. Let's be blunt. It's goddamn pedestrian."

"Yes, I agree. But I'm saying she's a fine painter. And I'm saying she'll be heard from."

"I trust racetrack touts more than anyone who predicts how an artist is going to do in the future. There ain't no future. Here is her work, right here on the wall, now. That's all we can deal with."

"You don't get it. All I'm saying is, without that creep around her neck any longer, she has to do better."

"If the two things have anything to do with each other . . . which I doubt."

"Do you doubt he was a creep?"

"I didn't know the man. I don't take any kind of bird artist seriously."

"Believe me, he was a creep. A four-star, knock-down-drag-out creep. A twisted, kinky old degenerate."

"You mean he liked to do it with great horned owls?"

The woman laughed and moved on; the man followed.

Lucy stood rooted to the spot, as though paralyzed.

I was a bit shaken myself. I had already heard some nasty things about Jack Carbondale—from Norma Hennion. He was cheap, she said, insensitive, and a slave driver.

And I had already intuited, given my medical and psychiatric training, that the Carbondale marriage was very close to a folie à deux ... although it was hard to tell which Carbondale was mad and which was mimicking the other's madness. But sexual perversion? Hardly.

Lucy's face was looking quite strange. The color had just drained out of it. Lucy was sophisticated. This was New York. There was almost no such thing as "kinky" in New York. Kinky was the norm.

I leaned over and said quietly to her, "Are you all right? You look as if you've seen the four horsemen of the apocalypse ... and one of them was riding a donkey."

She grasped my shoulder with such force that I twisted away from her.

I heard her savage whisper in return: "Don't you understand the horrible mistake we've made, Markus? We've ignored the garter. The garter in room 1502!"

Chapter 8

It was the strangest apartment I had ever stepped into, anywhere.

Moira Turk lived in a seven-room labyrinth with twisting hallways high above 116th Street at Riverside Drive, one block west of the Columbia University campus.

Moira was now a dressmaker, but for many years she had worked for the curator of the costume institute at the Metropolitan Museum of Art. As to how Lucy and she had met and become friends—that was never explained to me.

Moira was not a young woman, and her dressmaking seemed to have been taking a bizarre turn as of late; the garments hanging here and there in her apartment seemed appropriate for nineteenth-century ladies.

Anyway, after the requisite catching-up chat with Lucy, Miss Turk led us into a small, sparsely furnished office. She sat down behind the desk and slipped into her professional manner.

Lucy placed the garter on the desk . . . gently . . . with great deliberation . . . as if it were potentially explosive.

Moira Turk sort of scrunched down and glared at it for a while; then she picked it up and wound it around and around one finger, wearing it like a ring. Ultimately she dropped it back on the desktop.

"So what is it you want to know?" she asked. There was a pair of glasses on a chain around her neck, but I couldn't help wondering if they were mere decoration, because I had yet to see her put them on. She wore a large wristwatch, which she constantly consulted. She walked around in her apartment with an assortment of needles stuck in the shoulder of her dress. On the wall of that small room or office was a collection of antiquated measuring tapes.

When Lucy did not answer her question, Moira said, "On the phone you mentioned a murder."

"True," said Lucy.

"You can't strangle anything or anybody with this garter."

Well, at least Moira Turk had a sense of humor.

"I can't really tell you what I want to know. Or, rather, I want to know everything you can tell me about this garter."

Moira's grim face dissolved in laughter. "But Lucy, dear, what the hell are you talking about? A garter. Do you want a sartorial analysis? A historical analysis? Or do you want me to put it on?"

Then she looked at me for the first time; I mean, really looked at me. "And what is it that you want?" she asked.

"I want what Lucy wants."

"Very well, my friends. Here is what I will attempt to do. Situate this object in the history of costume."

She left the room and came back with an orange, which she began to peel over a sheet of newspaper. As she peeled she stared at the inert garter.

When the peeling was complete, she left the now naked fruit on the paper and began her garter investigation seriously.

She stretched the garter, sniffed it, made a tiny cut in it with a razor blade, threw it across the room and retrieved it, rubbed some kind of cream on it, put it on her forearm, and then went back to the orange and ate a single slice.

As she worked I had the strange feeling that I had been transported back in time and was watching Madame Curie in her laboratory.

A white cat wandered in, jumped onto the desk, inspected the garter and the fruit, jumped down again, and sauntered out.

"That was Lulu," Lucy informed me.

Moira Turk had one more orange section, then gave her analysis: "This is not a functional item. It appears to be simply the good old-fashioned circulation-stopping kind of thing that used to hold up our mothers' stockings. *Au contraire!* We are looking at only the *inside* of the thing. This garter had a covering, which has been stripped off. I think it was blue silk, or perhaps nylon. And it had two tassels—at least two. What you have brought me is a 'tossing' garter, Lucy."

"A what?"

Moira got up, did a quick and raucous parody of a bump and grind, and then pretended to fling something.

She sat back down. "Yes. Most likely it was a stripper's or a go-go dancer's. The kind that happy customers stick folded-up bills in along the girl's leg. The kind the dancer flings to the audience after a performance."

"My, my," Lucy said.

Ten minutes later we were standing on the west side of Riverside Drive waiting for the number 5 bus.

"What does it mean?" I asked Lucy.

"It means, Markus, that Carbondale did indeed have some peculiar tastes."

"Lucy, even I have some peculiar tastes."

"And, more important, it makes me think that Carbondale might really have been a denizen of that hotel . . . that he went there regularly to slake his peculiar thirsts. Maybe a couple of times a month."

"Even if he checked into the Hilton once a week, Lucy, the hotel management is not about to tell you that. We are not the police. They'll tell you nothing at the hotel."

"I'm fully aware of that fact, Markus."

She stepped out into the street and gazed uptown, looking, presumably, for the bus. Then she stepped back onto the sidewalk and said, "We are obviously unequipped to deal with the dark side of a great hotel."

"All hotels, Lucy, have dark sides. I mean, every night they host lonely people with money."

"An excellent observation. But the point is, dear Markus, who is qualified to advise us on the darkness?"

"The bellhops, the doormen, the parking attendants, the room service waiters. But they aren't talking. It's their livelihood. They don't make a living on their base pay."

"Keep your eye on the sparrow, Markus. I need a guide . . . not a lecture."

"Well, I don't know anyone."

"But I think you do."

"Who?"

"You once told me about a man who owns a bodega on 9th Avenue . . . just two blocks from your home."

"Oh, you mean Alfonso."

"Yes, that was his name. The Ecuadorian gangster."

"Wait a minute, Lucy. First of all, I don't know if he's from Ecuador. And I don't know that he's a gangster. And last, I haven't been in his place in years."

"But he is—how shall I put it?—shady."

"I suppose you could say he is," I admitted. Alfonso had been helpful to me once . . . very helpful. It was an incident that happened during the last year of my father's life. He had gotten ill again. I called the hospital. He was rushed by ambulance to St. Clare's on 9th Avenue. At some point his wallet was stolen. I didn't care about the credit cards, but I did care about the photos of my father and mother that he kept in the wallet. I mentioned the theft to my doorman, who suggested I contact this bodega owner on 9th Avenue—Alfonso. I went to see him and told him the story. Within a week the pictures, wrapped in wax paper, were returned to me with postage due. When I returned to the bodega to thank Alfonso, he denied having any hand in the recovery. So I didn't thank him any more; I just bought a hundred dollars worth of groceries, none of which I needed.

The bus came. We boarded.

As we worked our way to the back, Lucy asked, "Will you take me to him, Markus?"

Did I have an alternative?

Chapter 9

The three of us strolled into the bodega that afternoon. Three? Yes. I had decided to take my friend Duke, who was, after all, an underworld character. Retired and pensioned.

The bodega was still there, and friend Alfonso was exactly where I had left him, leaning against the low ice cream freezer, smoking a Newport, wearing a sports shirt over pressed brown pants. His shoes were highly shined, right down to the tips of the laces. He seemed ten years younger rather than ten years older.

As for the bodega itself—no change whatsoever. Shelves on either side—one side paper goods, the other side cans and packages of spaghetti.

In fact, it was a dazzling display of spaghetti

of every kind. The whole Ronzoni line from #1 to #11 and all points between and beyond.

The front of the store had a large, high counter behind which sat a woman selling cigarettes, Lotto tickets, and aspirin and ringing up the sales.

The floor was covered with false Greek tiles, morosely faded.

"Mr. Alfonso, it's good to see you again," I said.

Of course, I had no idea whether Alfonso was his first name or his last. He stared at the three of us. He said nothing.

"You once helped me out with a lost wallet. Years ago. It was my father's wallet. Someone stole it in the St. Clare's emergency room."

He replied in his strangely accented English. "Not me. I help no one."

Lucy butted in. "It's not your personal help we need. We need to find someone who . . . who . . ." And there she stopped, at a loss for words.

Finally, she simply said, "Look, Mr. Alfonso. We all know that hotel employees will supply guests with prostitutes if requested."

"People say that," Alfonso admitted.

"And it happens even at deluxe places like the Hilton."

"People say that," he repeated.

"In fact, a lot of strange peccadillos can be indulged."

"So I hear," he said. For the first time I noticed Alfonso's moustache and elegant little goatee. I couldn't recall if that had been his style ten years ago.

Lucy wrung her hands and went into one of her delicate Southern-damsel-in-distress routines.

It was so complex and shameless, particularly when she laid on the accent, that I cannot remember it verbatim.

But the content of the fable was that she had just arrived in New York from Tennessee to meet her long-lost cousin, who was staying at the Hilton. And before she could meet up with him, demon rum had taken his mind and he committed suicide. Now, she knows that a woman of the evening was in the room with him before he did that terrible thing. And she just wants to talk to the lady. And find out what he was thinking . . . and she wants to try to make some sense of the tragedy so that when she goes back home and tells his family, she can comfort them properly, giving them the entire story.

When she finished the tale she was weeping.

Alfonso, totally overwhelmed, became a gallant. He actually removed a folded handkerchief from his back pocket and wiped away some of her tears.

Then he stepped back and regarded us severely.

He pointed at Duke, who seemed quite happy.

"He has only three legs," Alfonso noted. I nodded, then knelt and began to console the pit bull about his disability.

Alfonso began to rock gently on his heels.

He said, "There's a bar on Eighth Avenue. It is called the Green Kettle. An old man gets drunk there. Every day. He used to park cars at the Plaza and the Hilton. His name is Bud Maddie. Don't say my name to him."

I purchased a large box of Milk Bones for Duke and we left.

Once out on the street, I said to Lucy, "That was unconscionable!"

"What?"

"That act you put on in there. I mean, yes, it

worked, Lucy. I'll give you that. But I found it very embarrassing."

"Aren't we the moralist?" she replied archly.

"I'm not criticizing your morals, Lucy. I'm—"

She cut me off by raising her hand like a crossing guard at the intersection. "You seem to have forgotten what I told you about the butcher bird."

"No, I haven't. I remember quite well. It was after Carbondale's body came hurtling down. You said, 'Beware the butcher bird.' "

"Very good, Markus. And one of the reasons I told you that was so you'd give it some thought."

"I have given it some thought. I'll give it more when I know what it means."

"Do you know why people dislike butcher birds so much, Markus?"

"No."

"Because they kill songbirds."

"Oh."

"But falcons and hawks also kill songbirds, don't they?"

"Yes."

"Do people hate falcons and hawks?"

"No, I don't suppose they do."

"Yet the butcher bird is hated. Now we do

know that butcher birds sometimes hang their victims on thorns, and we do know that they occasionally kill just to eat the brain of a bird they consider a delicacy. Markus, there are many predators who do the same. Bird and mammal and insect. But people *hate* the butcher bird. Do you know why?"

"I've already told you I don't know; besides, *I* don't hate the butcher bird. And what does this have to do with my comments about what you did in the bodega?"

"People hate the butcher bird, Markus, because it doesn't look like a predator. In fact, it looks like a larger version of the very songbird it kills. Now do you see my point?"

This was always a problem. She was a bit too deep for me.

"Maybe we should call it a day, Lucy," I said, "and go to that bar tomorrow."

She shriveled me with one look. I should have expected it. It was that bird-watcher's steely glare, which says, "I will climb the highest mountain, walk through the fires of hell, or go to the North Pole with one blanket and an apple for a single good sighting."

So all we did was dump Duke back into his bedroom, open the box of Milk Bones for him, have a cup of tea, nap for half an hour (on separate beds, of course), and start out again.

It was growing dark. But believe me, the day was not yet over. In fact, it had just begun.

As we headed toward the bar called the Green Kettle on 8th Avenue, I had an inkling of trouble. Lucy was definitely in her birder walk mode—moving fast and light with the shoulders slightly hunched and the head tilted ever so subtly to refract the sun's rays, if there were any.

Usually Lucy's birder walk sent me into paroxysms of further affection for her. Not that evening. There were no birds where we were going. Except maybe a vulture or two.

The establishment had large, dirty windows on the street. We peered in.

Some twenty men in various stages of decrepitude and inebriation were drinking at the very long bar. Two bartenders were in evidence.

The tables opposite the bar area were empty. Situated next to them, close to the door, was a hot food counter, which had obviously been closed down for the day.

Lucy touched me on the shoulder. "Was this the type of place you used to frequent, Markus, when you were a dissolute young medical student?"

"I was never dissolute. But whatever I was, I wouldn't have set foot into a place like this."

"Too dangerous?"

"No. Depressing."

"It is the blight man was born for," she philosophized.

"You didn't say that when we went into that place in SoHo—Fanelli's," I retorted cynically.

"You are missing the point."

"The point being what—demon rum?" I chided. Lucy winced a little. My beloved was the most sophisticated of ladies, but deep, deep down there was a violent Bible Belt prejudice in her against alcohol, even though she often, as they say, imbibed.

Anyway, the interesting and dangerous conversation was aborted when Lucy walked through the barroom door. I followed.

We slid into a spot at the front of the bar. All the stools were taken. The bartender—a large man with big red hands and a round, protruding stomach—played with a bar rag and watched us intently.

He was neither friendly nor unfriendly.

Rather, he looked as if he had suddenly been accosted by aliens.

Finally, he seemed to decide that we were just folks—strange folks—who wanted a drink.

He wiped the bar in front of Lucy, threw down two cardboard coasters, and said, "What can I get ya?"

"I need a minute of your time," she answered.

He grunted out a strange little laugh, stepped back and looked at us . . . then shook out his rag with a flourish.

The man seated next to me, dressed in a faded army fatigue jacket and drinking beer from a long-necked bottle, began to chuckle.

The bartender said, "Sure, lady. No problem. A minute of my time? I got plenty of minutes. Take all the minutes you want. Minutes and minutes."

"I am looking for a gentleman called Bud Maddie."

The bartender's eyes opened wide. "Then you came to the wrong place," he said.

"Why?"

"Because Bud Maddie is no longer with us. Because Bud is with the angels now."

"You mean Mr. Maddie is dead?"

"Dead as the last rose of summer, lady."

"Are you sure?" Lucy pressed.

"Would I lie to you?" He rolled his eyes and looked around. Then he walked over to the dazed-looking old man who sat a few stools down the line.

The bartender shook him. "Did you hear that? Tell her. She thinks I'm lying to her."

"Buddie's with the angels," the old drunk slurred.

The bartender turned back to Lucy with a big grin on his face. "See?"

Lucy went boldly over to the old man and stood just behind his shoulder. He did not turn around. He was drinking rye whiskey, straight; a stein of ice water stood next to his whiskey glass. An unfiltered Pall Mall lay burning in the chipped ashtray near his wrist. Though he sat quietly, I could hear his laboring lungs. He was a small man, but his face was thick and creased. He wore a tan-colored beret.

"When did Mr. Maddie pass away?" Lucy asked.

He did not answer.

"Please," she said, "it's very important."

The old man stood up so suddenly that Lucy jumped back and banged into me.

"He died just now!" the man shouted. Then he drained his whiskey in one gulp and faked a collapse onto the bar.

The room exploded with laughter at his performance. The man lifted his head and acknowledged the praise with a Churchillian wave of the hand.

That poor old fellow. He should have known better than to trifle with Lucy Wayles.

She beckoned the bartender with a crook of her finger. "What is the dead man drinking?"

"Fleischmann's," he said.

"I'll have some too."

"Some," he repeated simply.

"A triple, to be precise. Straight up. With ice water on the side."

Then she looked at me. "Pay the man, Markus."

I took out a twenty and placed it on top of the bar. I had no idea what a triple Fleischmann's cost.

The bartender placed the drink in front of Lucy. He took my twenty dollars and gave me ten in change.

Lucy, smiling now, picked up the glass in one hand and the stein of water in the other and literally waved them under the old man's nose. "Shall we continue this conversation at a table, Mr. Maddie—where you can drink in peace?"

It was too delectable a carrot to refuse. The old man shuffled after us and we all sat at one of the sea of empty tables.

Lucy pushed the drink in front of him. "I would prefer it if you did not smoke," she said.

He lit another Pall Mall.

"Are you the same Bud Maddie who used to park cars at the Hilton and the Plaza?"

He exhaled, enveloping us in smoke. "I did a helluva lot more than just park cars, my friend. And I worked a helluva lot more hotels."

He began to drink, staring at Lucy over the rim of the glass. When he at last took a breather, he looked warily at me. "You with the cops?" he asked.

It was, frankly, given my age, a compliment.

"No, certainly not," I said.

"With the union?"

"No."

"From the state?"

What did he mean by that? "No."

"Well, then, what is it?" He was directing his words to Lucy now. "You going to sell me a church raffle?"

"No."

"So what the hell do you want, bothering a respectable man like myself?"

Lucy opened her purse and pulled out two items. She laid them on the table in front of Bud Maddie.

One was the back flap of a recent Carbondale field guide, with a fairly recent author photo.

The other was an article cut from an issue of the *News* reporting on Carbondale's suicide and containing an early photograph of him.

"Please look these over," Lucy said, pushing the two sheets next to Maddie's drink.

The old man's eyes lit up. "Hell, I read that already. I knew the costume man killed himself. Poor bastard."

"What did you call him?" Lucy demanded.

The old man pushed the papers back across the table.

"What was it that you said?" she asked again. "You called him a name. Something about a costume."

Bud Maddie leaned back in his chair. He took off his beret, brushed it for lint, and replaced it gingerly. Between the taking it off and the putting it on again, his entire expression changed radically. He obviously had reevaluated the situation. He was no longer frightened or confused by this strange couple. Now he was on familiar ground. There were buyers and there were sellers and he knew which was which.

Lucy turned to me. "Why don't you get another drink for Mr. Maddie?"

I went to the bar and ordered—a double this time—and headed back toward the table with it.

Maddie called out: "And some potato chips." I turned back, purchased the chips, and hurried to the table with all the refreshments.

"Why did you call him the costume man?" Lucy was asking as I sat down. "Did he wear a disguise of some sort?"

Silent, he laboriously began to open the bag of chips.

"Please, Markus, help our friend Mr. Maddie."

I grabbed the bag, ripped it open, and gave it back to him.

"It is very important that you talk to me," Lucy said.

The old man smiled. "Here's what I got to talk about. It's going to be a long winter, ain't it? And me—with just Social Security and a pension that wouldn't keep a wharf rat in cheese. So I think I'm gonna need something to make it warm. You know what I mean? Something to make the apartment cozy. Yeah. Like a Sony fourteen-inch color TV."

He ate one potato chip.

Lucy glared at him. But when she did respond, it was in a very controlled voice.

"Are you saying to us, Mr. Maddie, that if we obtain one of these television sets for you, you will tell us everything you know about the 'costume man,' as you call him?"

"Yep."

"Very well." She turned to me. "Markus, will you please go and purchase Mr. Maddie the set he wants."

"Now!"

Lucy looked at the old man and then nodded. "Yes," she said. "Now."

"But the stores are closed, Lucy. I can't just go out and buy a television, as if it were a frankfurter."

Maddie said helpfully, "The Wiz on Sixth Avenue is open till ten."

I was trapped, furious, incredulous. Did Lucy really expect me to do this, or was it some kind of ploy? If it was the latter, she gave me no clue as to what the ploy was.

"We'll be waiting right here for you, Markus."

I went out into the night. This was going to go down in the books as one of my most memorable and preposterous adventures; I could feel it. It was hard enough to find the electronics emporium. It was harder getting the model number of the set Maddie had demanded, and harder still to haul the unwieldy carton out to the street all alone. The single most difficult part, though, was flagging down a cab to take the Sony and me back to the Green Kettle.

An hour and twenty minutes later, the old man, Lucy, I, and the Sony were at the same table.

"I gotta see it open and playing," demanded Maddie.

"Please, Markus . . ." Lucy said.

I uncrated the damn thing and plugged it into the wall socket nearby. Using the remote control, I switched to channel eleven. A Hercules movie was just starting, or perhaps ending.

"Okay," Bud Maddie said. He signaled that I should turn off the set and recrate it. I did so. I was, by now, totally exhausted. I slumped over, inert.

"Why do you call him costume man? What kind of costume did he wear?" Lucy asked Maddie once more.

"We didn't know what he wore. We never actually saw him in a costume. We called him that because of the broad who used to visit him. Every time he checked in, she paid him a call. And she always carried these dry cleaning bags with some kind of costumes in them— you could see the feathers through the plastic. So whatever went on in his room, one of them probably put the feathers on. Stands to reason, don't it?"

"Did he check in often?"

"Like clockwork. At least twice a month. He always tried to get the same room. And that same woman always showed up, lugging that feathered stuff."

"Was she a known prostitute?"

"Who said she was a prostitute? All I know about her I heard from one of the valets. He said she was a dancer in a topless joint downtown. On Tenth Avenue. It's called the Turret."

"Do you know this woman's name?"

"No."

"What did she look like? Describe her."

"Short blond hair. Not a kid. About thirty-five maybe. And she talked with a weird accent."

"What kind of accent?"

"I don't know. Maybe Russian."

"What do you think happened in that room, Mr. Maddie?"

"I think they put on the costumes."

"And then what?"

"And then they did a lot of stuff that simply ain't for a lady's ears."

Maddie's efforts at gallantry roused me. I looked at Lucy. She was radiant.

"You've been most helpful, Mr. Maddie," she said. "I do hope your new television set brings you great pleasure."

I would have liked to drop it on the old man's head from a great height.

Lucy and I walked outside and stood in front of the Green Kettle. The weather was turning cold.

"Did you pay cash, Markus?"

"No. I used a credit card."

"Good. You may be able to deduct it at income tax time as a legitimate business expense."

"I don't have a business, Lucy. I'm retired."

"You're quibbling, Markus. Please hail a cab."

"I take it we are proceeding downtown."

"Correct. The trail is too hot now to make camp and pitch our tent. We are no longer merely bird-watchers, Markus. We are now field ornithologists, and we are going deeper and deeper into the jungle to find the rarest of birds."

Oh?

I got a cab.

The Turret was a "lounge" situated where 10th Avenue begins—or ends—all the way downtown. It was, I suppose, the Cadillac of nude-dancing establishments. Well, almost nude. Every woman who danced there maintained one item of fabric on her body at all times.

There was no cover—to employ a wicked pun—and no minimum, but the moment you were seated either at one of the horseshoe bars or at a table, it was made clear that you must order a drink for ten dollars, no matter what you drank. And you had to reorder at reasonable intervals.

We were guided to a table by a man who looked like Mr. Clean—huge, bald, and sporting one earring. He was wearing, of all things, a tuxedo and sneakers. On the lapel of his jacket was an identification badge: MY NAME IS DARBY.

He graciously held the chair for Lucy and then vanished, to be replaced almost immediately by a "waitress," a young lady in an evening gown. That was one of the oddities of the place, I realized: conflicting signals. The garb of the staff was the sort of thing you might see in a swank nightclub, but there was sawdust on the floor, giving the place the illusion of a college town alehouse.

Lucy ordered an abstemious ginger ale. I asked for a vodka with grapefruit juice.

Lucy looked around boldly. "This is the first time I have ever been in such an establishment," she confided in a hushed voice.

I had been in several. But that was years ago, and the subject is probably best left unexplored.

There was only one dancer onstage: a tall, thin girl with long blond tresses and a remarkably ample bosom. What garments she had on were of American Indian style. I guess her "shtick" was to be an erotic Pocahontas. She was dancing slowly to languorous disco music.

There were not many customers in the audience. A table of Japanese businessmen. Two Italian naval officers at the bar. Several single occupied tables with refugee Wall Streeters. A bar contingent of middle-aged men who were obviously at the tail end of some kind of military reunion. Maybe Korea. Maybe Vietnam. One wore a baseball cap with the insignia of the First Cav.—yellow and black. There was a lot of cigarette smoke. Each table had a huge ashtray and several tiny boxes of wooden matches with the lovely Turret logo on the top of each box—like Camelot.

"I love this kind of matches," Lucy said, slipping several of the boxes sheepishly into her purse.

Lucy was in fact the only woman in the audience.

"Tell me, Markus. Do you find that woman on the stage enticing?"

"How do you mean that, Lucy?"

"Let's not beat around the bush. Does she excite you sexually?"

"You are the only one who excites me in that manner," I replied.

Lucy sipped her ginger ale and gave me one of her sly looks—which could mean anything. And I do mean *anything*.

But out of deference to her curiosity I did begin to study that young dancer critically.

My concentration was broken when I heard Lucy call out, "Young man! Young man!"

She was paging Mr. Clean. He approached the table smiling and positioned himself between Lucy and myself.

"Am I correct in assuming that you are a bouncer as well as the maître d'?"

He seemed to contemplate the question for a long time. Then he replied, still very gracious, "We rarely require that kind of thing here. But I will perform security functions if required."

"And your name . . . how is it pronounced?"

"The way it is spelled."

"But the English pronounce 'Derby' as 'Darby.' "

"Yes, ma'am. But my name is Darby to begin with. D-A-R-B-Y, not D-E-R-B-Y."

"Yes, of course it is. How silly of me. Is the blond woman dancing tonight?" Lucy asked.

Oh! She had slipped that in beautifully. Elegantly.

"That's a blond woman dancing now,"

Darby replied. Nothing seemed to surprise or unbalance this young man—I had to give him that.

"Oh, this one is older. A bit heavier. She speaks with an accent."

"You mean Genya?"

"Yes, of course."

"No. She has two days off."

"How can I reach her?"

"I'm sorry, we give out no personal information on our performers."

"An intelligent policy," Lucy agreed. "A man with inflamed passions is not to be trusted. My aunt Hattie once said she didn't know anything about the animal kingdom until her wedding night."

Darby, a.k.a. Mr. Clean, smiled and wandered off. I think he wanted to be out of Lucy's earshot when he broke into unbridled laughter.

"Go back to your studies," Lucy said to me. I obeyed.

Then I heard that refrain again. "Young man! Young man!"

What was she up to now?

Mr. Clean arrived again, still gracious.

"Would you take a seat for a moment?" Lucy asked him.

"Why?"

"I want to show you something."

He sat down.

"How is your eyesight, Mr. Darby?"

"Passable."

"That's good."

Then, to my astonishment, she removed one of her small earrings and placed it on the table in front of him. "Do you know what this is?"

"An earring," he answered without hesitating.

"Yes. But look at the intricate design worked into the silver."

The young man sighed, as if it was too late to escape, leaned over, and examined the earring.

"I'm afraid my eyes aren't *that* good. I can't make out any design," he said.

"Yes. It is hard to see, isn't it? But let me describe it. On this small earring is a masked duck in flight."

"That's nice."

"I am one of the few bird-watchers on the northeast coast who can point to a masked duck on my life list. It is a tropical bird, you see, that has only recently begun to move north. And it is a very secretive bird, Mr. Darby—almost like a rail."

This thing with the masked duck was so outside the young man's realm of experience that he couldn't respond at all.

Lucy was not pleased. She continued her outlandish presentation.

"Now, my daughter is getting married shortly. The day after Thanksgiving, in fact. I asked her what she wanted as a gift. She said she wanted these earrings."

Lucy then suddenly reached across the table and pressed the hand of the young host like a funeralgoer comforting the bereaved. "But I can't give the earrings to her. I can't, because these are made for pierced ears and my daughter's ears are not pierced."

Darby didn't know how to respond to this either.

Lucy pulled her hand away. "And that's why I have to contact Genya," she said. "She made these earrings."

"You're kidding."

"No, I'm not. She's the only one who can make another pair, for nonpierced ears this time."

Darby pushed the earring about a bit on the

table, gently, with his huge hand. "Incredible," he said. "I never knew Genya Markov was into that kind of stuff."

Bingo! Lucy had now wormed Genya's last name out of Mr. Clean. What a perform-ance. . . .

Darby then stood quickly. "Okay. I don't want your daughter to be disappointed. Genya lives on Downing Street. I don't know the exact address. But it's a crumbling blue house just east of Seventh. With a stoop."

"Blue?" I queried.

"Yes," he said. "That's the color of the house. Blue."

"Thank you," Lucy said. "And my daughter would thank you too if she were here."

He left us then. Lucy leaned over and pulled my ear ever so delicately. "Believe me, Markus, if I did have a daughter and she was about to be married, you would be invited."

She then restored the earring to its rightful place—her own precious earlobe.

Even in the bleak, cold night, we could see that Darby had not fantasized. There was a blue house where he said it would be. And it had a crumbling blue stoop.

Lucy took my hand as we stared at the tumbledown building.

"We have come a long way," she said, "through desert and jungle. And now, Markus, we have reached the nesting site."

We walked up the stairs and into the tiny hallway, which was in dire need of repair.

According to the panel of doorbells, a G. Markov lived in apartment 3R. There were two bells for each floor—*F* for "front" apartments and *R* for "rear." There was no name listed for 3F.

Lucy leaned on the bell. My fatigue had vanished. The chase was now too intense.

There was no response whatsoever.

Lucy tried the inside door. Locked.

"Ring all the bells," I suggested.

She did so, employing her ten-finger technique.

In a minute an enraged man flung the inside door open and began to scream at us. "What are you doing out here? Who the hell are you?" he demanded.

Lucy soon placated him and pleaded to be allowed in to see her dear friend Genya Markov, who for some reason wasn't answering the bell, and Lucy was getting "a little worried about her."

Another victory for Lucy. He seemed to swallow the story whole, and he suddenly turned most helpful. "She probably didn't hear you ring," he explained patiently. "Looks like she's moving out. A guy brought up a lot of cartons a while ago."

He moved aside and let us enter. "Thank you so much," Lucy said. "Third floor in the back, wasn't it?"

"That's right. There's only one occupied apartment on that floor."

When we reached the third-floor landing and turned toward the rear apartment, we saw the moving cartons stacked on either side of us. A dolly blocked the open door to 3R.

Lucy pulled the dolly aside, stepped tentatively inside, and called out: "Miss Markov?"

No answer.

"Genya? Genya Markov!"

No answer.

We walked into the apartment entrance, a small, dimly lit alcove.

Lucy went into the living room, a left turn out of the alcove. In the center of the room was a beautiful highback sofa that seemed to have been stolen right out of a boudoir in the Sun King's palace.

A woman was seated at one end, resting her head on the sofa arm.

"I didn't mean to barge in like this," Lucy said, abashed.

But there was no need for that apology.

Genya Markov appeared to be resting, but she was in truth dead. We could see the clotted blood down her neck and bosom. The woman's throat had been slashed.

Lucy sat down beside her.

"Why is there no blood on the sofa, Markus?"

"I guess because she was killed elsewhere and moved here after the blood had clotted."

"Did you ever see anything so sad?" Lucy cried. She was speaking to no one in particular.

For some reason, stumbling upon the body this way, all I could think was that if this dead woman was Genya Markov—and it appeared, based on the description we had been given, that she was—then I definitely would not have paid to see her dance. That is really what was going through my head.

"What type of weapon was it that killed her?" Lucy asked.

The wounds were clearly visible. Several slashes on both sides of the throat.

"Looks like a razor blade—or a scalpel," I said.

"Or an X-Acto knife from Jack Carbondale's studio," she declared.

"Yes, it could be that," I admitted, realizing that Lucy was now beginning to speculate.

"Call the police, Markus."

I went to the phone and dialed 911.

"Hurry now, Markus. We have to conduct a search before they arrive."

"That would be illegal," I protested.

"Search, Doctor!"

"For what, Lucy?"

"Whatever."

She bolted up from the sofa. "Look there."

Stuck into the sides of a mirror were a group of bad snapshots of Genya Markov. Some showed her in ballet costume. Some in the costume of a figure skater. Some in evening clothes. None of her in the Turret.

Lucy studied the photos carefully. "Get that big closet, Markus!" she ordered, still sifting through the pictures.

I walked to the closet and slid the door open on its railing. My eyes were hit by an astonishing profusion of color . . . so strong that I involuntarily made a kind of croaking noise.

Lucy rushed over to me. "Are you in cardiac arrest, Markus?"

All I could do was point. My God, the costumes!

Lucy followed my finger. She pushed the hangers apart to get a better look. Then she plucked one off the pole.

"Do you remember this?" she asked, displaying it.

I looked at her blankly.

"Think, Markus," she prompted. "We were together somewhere when you saw this costume. Remember?"

"Not really. You tend to dress better than that, Lucy."

"Don't be stupid. I mean at the ballet. Two years ago."

"Firebird! It's a firebird costume," I blurted out, finally seeing the light.

She pulled out another one. "And this seems to suggest a bluebird."

She lifted a third outfit from the ranks. "This one looks to be from the dying swan scene. Yes . . . all costumes from ballets with allegorical avians."

I turned suddenly to look at the corpse. Then back at the costume. "Lucy, what is an allegorical avian?"

"Don't bother me now with questions, Markus."

It wasn't the question I really wanted to ask anyhow. What really confused me was the activity that might or might not have occurred in room 1502. Genya Markov visits Jack Wesley Carbondale again and again in his hotel room over the years. She always carries costumes in with her. Does she dance for Carbondale in those costumes? Does he do the dancing? What sort of sex transpires?

Of course, what did it really matter? Both dancers—dancers, lovers, perverts, explorers, whatever—were now dead.

And the police were at the front door.

Chapter 10

Lucy has a way with cops, to put it colloquially.

She wasn't in the least disturbed when after a short time with several detectives in that apartment it became clear the NYPD considered us—Lucy and me—prime suspects.

The homicide detectives were particularly skeptical of her earring story, the same one she had told Darby in the Turret—that she was seeking Genya Markov's services as a jeweler.

After the body was taken away and the crime scene analyzed and the neighbors interviewed and the moving cartons dusted for prints, the department brought in what was obviously its best interrogator: one Detective Bilboa.

By that time Lucy and I were ensconced in

the small Markov kitchen at a white Formica table.

I had already suggested to Lucy that she stop all the nonsense about earrings and just tell the police what she had learned about Carbondale and Genya Markov and the whole mess.

Lucy turned on me savagely and told me to keep my mouth shut and my eyes open.

And then in came Detective Bilboa. He was wearing one of those athletic jackets. And he had a great deal of beautifully combed black hair.

The first thing he said to us was, "She was Ukrainian, not Russian."

Then he proceeded in a rather absent-minded fashion to open and close every cupboard in the kitchen.

"Were you aware that she was Ukrainian?" he asked.

"Whom are you addressing?" Lucy asked sharply.

"Both of you."

"Neither of us was aware of that fact," Lucy asserted. She was not lying there. We thought she was a Russian. Anyway, she couldn't have been a recent émigré.

Detective Bilboa then opened the refrigerator door and peered intently at the contents. He pulled out a loaf of wrapped bread—a variety of pumpernickel—and sniffed at it tentatively. Then he checked the freshness-expiration date.

"Why do people insist on keeping bread in the refrigerator? It doesn't keep the bread fresh, you know. That's a common delusion. You're better off leaving it out, allowing it to go stale, and then toasting it."

He stared directly at Lucy. "Do you agree with me?"

"Absolutely," she affirmed.

There was some kind of game going on between them, but I couldn't pick up on the rules or the point of it.

Detective Bilboa put the loaf back into the fridge. He dug into his pockets and came up with the driver's licenses we had proffered as identification when the police had first arrived. He handed the plasticized licenses back to us.

"Tell me again," he said, "what you did in the apartment after you found the body."

"Did?" Lucy repeated. "We did nothing. We called the police . . . obviously."

"You didn't find anything?"

"Nothing."

"And you didn't disturb anything?"

"Of course not."

"And there was no sign of a weapon?"

"No, none."

"Tell me . . . would either of you . . . object . . . to a body search?"

"Whose body are you—?" I began asking.

But Lucy did not allow me to finish.

She snapped out the words: "I would object, young man. Strenuously."

And I could see her hands begin to tremble with rage. She folded and unfolded them. I knew what was happening—delayed shock. When I was very young and worked the ER at Coney Island Hospital in Brooklyn—before deciding to go into medical research—I saw it every day in the relatives of patients. A young boy and his elder brother are bike riding. The younger child is hit by a car. His brother coolly and almost expertly delivers him to the emergency room, where the medical staff ministers to the injured boy. Someone asks the brother if he wants a glass of water. He collapses. Delayed shock.

Yes, Lucy was only now reacting to that slashed corpse on the sofa.

She started to rant a bit. "You don't know who you're dealing with, Detective. You must think we are vagrants. I'll have you know that I have received commendations from three mayors of this city—possibly four—for my work in setting up the most extensive library in the country dealing with urban natural history. People come to New York City from all over the world in order to consult it. Do you understand? Even from Zaire. And this man here, Dr. Markus Bloch? He has done more to help humankind understand the invidious nature of the cold virus than . . ."

My accomplishments slowed her down for a moment. But then she switched gears.

"Search us? For what? You spoke to the man who let us in. I know that. He confirmed our time of entry into the building. You know Genya Markov was dead long before we climbed those stairs."

I decided it was time to intervene in a humorous way, in order to defuse the rapidly escalating situation.

I stood up and announced: "You can strip-search me." And I fairly shouted, "The New

York Police Department can have all of me!"
Then I did a pathetic imitation of a bump and
grind.

My clowning accomplished nothing other
than stunned silence. But at least Lucy seemed
to regain a measure of control.

Detective Bilboa wagged a finger at Lucy.
"The more I look at you," he said, "the more I
think I've seen you somewhere before."

She twitted him in her gun moll style. "I
have a rap sheet as long as your arm. Two con-
victions on assault, three for gun possession,
one for manslaughter."

Ah, now she was back in form, although she
never could get the accent just right.

Bilboa was not put off. "I've got it. That's it.
I saw you on television. What was it—a year
or two ago. Something about a bird on a
bridge."

I helped out. "The bird was a tufted duck.
The bridge was at Fifty-ninth Street."

"Yeah. Now I remember. You were all over
the place for a while. I remember the announcer saying, 'You've heard of the Bird Man
of Alcatraz. Well, we have the Bird Woman of
Roosevelt Island.' "

"That announcer misspoke," I put in. "The

Roosevelt Island tram runs *under* the bridge.
Lucy rescued the duck from a girder on the
bridge itself. And she was arrested on the
Queens side of the bridge—not on Roosevelt
Island."

"Sure, sure," Bilboa said. "Whatever you
say." He had suddenly lost interest in Lucy's
heroics. He ran the water in the sink and took
down a glass from the cabinet. "You people
are free to go," he said after drinking, addressing the empty glass but obviously meaning us.

We both stood.

He raised a hand then, signifying that there
was something more he had to tell us.

And there was.

"I don't believe a word of what either of you
told us. I don't know why you were in this
apartment. I don't really know who the hell
you are or what your game is. But we'll be
watching you. Do you understand?"

We each nodded and walked slowly out of
the apartment. We walked down the stairs
even more slowly.

"You may lean on me, Markus," Lucy said.

Did I really look that bad? That feeble? Well,
it *had* been just about the longest night of my
life.

When the taxi dropped me off I turned, briefly, to call back to Lucy, "Why didn't you tell them?"

The cab driver was anxious to move on. He gave me a dirty look. But I remained there on the sidewalk, holding the back door open.

"Tell them what, Markus? Tell who, what?"

"You know what I mean, Lucy. About Genya Markov and Carbondale and . . . 1502."

She leaned toward the open door and patted me on the hand. "I wasn't asked," she said. "Now, you must go upstairs and get a very good night's sleep, Markus."

Lucy pulled the door shut. The cab drove off. I went up to my apartment and fell onto my bed. I was asleep within seconds.

I awoke about 3:00 A.M. to find myself fully dressed. I got into my pajamas and flopped down again. I was a tired man.

This time I dreamed. It was a lovely dream: Lucy and I were visiting the glittering cities of Europe. In each place I was invited to the opera house and introduced as "the greatest male dancer ever produced by America." I was greeted with wild applause, and the audience demanded that I perform.

So I did—after gaining Lucy's proud approval.

My act was a reverie striptease done to music written for me by Stravinsky himself.

Instead of taking off clothes, I put on feathers, and at the end of the performance I was a brilliant bird of paradise.

The audience brought me back for no fewer than five encores and carpeted the stage with roses.

I woke from that dream lying on my side, staring at the clock.

It was only seven-thirty. I rolled over and tried to sleep again. Maybe I could re-immerse myself in that strangely wonderful dream. Maybe the "tour" would continue . . . I would become the toast of all Asia.

Suddenly I was face to face with a horrendous gargoyle of a visage.

I cried out in horror, grabbed the pillow to protect myself, and started to clamber out of bed.

Then I realized it was Duke's face I was staring at.

"What the hell are you doing on my bed?" I asked, ashamed of my reaction.

He groaned.

Then I realized someone was knocking persistently at my door.

Immediately I thought, It must be Lucy. A stranger would have rung the lobby bell. Only Lucy, whom the doorman knew, was allowed up unannounced.

But why would she be here at this hour? It had to be trouble. She was supposed to sleep all day after that night of guys and dolls and molls and cops and corpses.

"Get off the bed, Duke," I ordered. Then I put on my father's old terry-cloth beach robe, which functioned as my bathrobe, rushed to the door, and opened it.

Lucy was not there. Two young boys were. They stood side by side, the shorter one a redhead, the taller one with black hair.

They were dressed in the strangest fashion. Both wore baseball caps with the bill at the back rather than the front of the head. Both wore baggy blue jeans that rode so low on the hips I thought it only a matter of time before they dropped around the boys' ankles. The smaller boy had on a thick hooded sweatshirt with a Chicago Bulls logo emblazoned across the chest. The taller one was in an antique

Brooklyn Dodgers baseball jacket with "1955" stitched on the breast.

"I'm Jake," said the smaller one.

"I'm Albert," the other one said.

I stared at them, confused.

"Aren't you Uncle Markus?" Albert asked.

Oh, Lord! I had forgotten all about my nephews—actually my grandnephews.

I didn't know what to say, so I said, "Was the plane on time?"

"Yep," said Jake, "but after we took off from Chicago—ten minutes after we took off—we hit a storm."

"No storm," corrected his brother loftily. "It was just turbulence."

"Yep," said Jake, adjusting his description so as not to alienate his older brother.

"They lost our luggage," Albert said.

"Yep," Jake echoed.

And then both boys burst out laughing and slapped palms, their arms held high in the air. I knew from watching televised sports events that this gesture was called the "high five." I knew they were nine and eleven years old, respectively, but, even considering their ages, I could not understand why anyone would be happy at the airline's loss of his bags.

"You had better call your parents," I said and ushered the children in.

Albert made the call while Jake, close by, monitored it.

"Dad says hello," Albert reported after he hung up.

It was then that Duke wandered, or rather hopped, into the living room. The dog stared at the boys and they at him.

"Daddy didn't tell us you had a dog," said Jake.

"I guess I forgot to tell him."

"He only has three legs," Albert noted.

"That is correct."

"He's ugly," Jake said.

"That is also correct." Then I modified my assent slightly. "Actually, as pit bulls go, he's quite handsome."

"What happened to his leg?" Albert asked, keeping his voice at a discreet whisper, as if not wanting to offend Duke.

"It was shot off."

"Wow! Like in a gunfight?"

"So I'm told."

"Cool . . . a gangsta dog!" Albert exclaimed. He and his little brother exchanged high fives again.

Duke then made the decision that Jake and Albert were his kind of people. He flopped down heavily from his three-point stance and rolled over on his back.

"What's he doing?" Jake asked.

"I don't know," I had to admit. In fact, I had never seen Duke do anything like that before. But then again, he had never tried to wake me before, either.

"He wants to be scratched," Albert announced.

"Yep," said Jake.

The boys sat down beside the beast and proceeded with the scratching. To hear a pit bull groan with pleasure is like hearing Attila the Hun squeal at the sight of a beautifully formed tiny musk rose.

While they were engaged with pleasuring Duke, I asked them questions about the loss of their luggage.

It turned out they had each been carrying only a knapsack.

"Why did you check them, then? Why didn't you carry them on the plane with you?"

My question was an intelligent one, I thought. It produced only evasion. After more probing, I finally got the truth out of them.

They checked their knapsacks because they wanted to go to the luggage pickup site after the flight landed. Why? Because they got a kick watching the bags spin down the chute with all the tags attached.

God bless the young. I went to my desk and retrieved the sheet of paper on which I had written their arrival and departure dates and other relevant data. Then I called the airline. I was informed that the knapsacks were now in Boston. Once they were routed back to New York they would be delivered to me, at no charge naturally.

I put down the phone and tried to think what to do next.

Of course. Breakfast. I had to feed Jake and Albert. Then I had to replace whatever essentials they had in their errant bags. Toothbrushes? Hand-held video games? Comics? Fresh socks? I had no idea what children considered essentials. Then I had to take them around New York City. They would only be here for a few days.

Oh, there was lots to do. But I knew damn well the only thing I was going to do after breakfast was to bring them over to Lucy's. She was my guide in affairs of state.

We went to McDonald's on 8th Avenue. The boys ate hugely.

Albert, halfway through his second Egg Mc-Muffin, inquired, "Are you too old to be my uncle?"

"I'm not really your uncle."

"What are you?"

"I guess I'm your great-uncle. I mean, your father's father was my brother. Your father is my real nephew."

"Then who's my real uncle?"

"You don't have one."

Jake looked as if he were about to burst into tears.

"But you have a real aunt," I hastened to add. "Your father has a sister."

"Yep!" Jake admitted happily.

"And after we eat we'll go to see another aunt."

"What aunt?" Albert asked.

"This is a great-aunt, twice removed. Aunt Lucy."

My analysis was beginning to confuse them. They concentrated on their food.

After breakfast we took the long walk through the park up to Lucy's apartment.

When she opened the door it was obvious I

had roused her from a sound sleep. She was angry, until she saw Jake and Albert and their backwards baseball caps and baggy pants.

"I know who you people are!" she fairly shouted and pulled them inside.

Her big cat, Dipper, however, did not share her enthusiasm. He took one look at the Chicago "rappers" and leaped and climbed to the top of the highest bookcase, where he glowered down, tail moving from side to side like a radar dish.

"Oh, don't mind him," Lucy said.

"It's a lynx," Jake noted. "I saw one in a zoo once."

Lucy whispered in my ear: "Given the circumstances, Markus, I am authorizing a three-day leave of absence from Olmsted's Irregulars during the coming week."

I whispered back: "Thank you, *mon generale*."

She stepped back and said in a loud voice, "Now I have to dress, Markus. You make the hot chocolate for the boys. I'll only be a little while. Then we'll figure out an itinerary."

There she goes again, I thought. Always giving me orders to make hot chocolate or cocoa or something like that when she knows damn well I can't.

Lucy vanished into the bedroom.

Actually, there was no need to do anything for the boys. They seemed to be fascinated by the unique clutter of Lucy's apartment—stacks of books and magazines all about, garish bird prints on the walls, strange wood carvings.

They wandered about like explorers in a new land, once in a while knocking over a pile in their exuberance.

Lucy came out of her bedroom in five minutes. Oh, how lovely she looked. She was wearing a dressed-up version of her basic birder outfit, including her boots and the hippie headband.

"Well," she said, "I think the first order of business is for your Uncle Markus to take you on a boat ride. The Circle Line is the finest boat ride around the finest city in the world."

"The Bulls beat the Knicks all the time," Jake retorted.

Lucy hadn't the slightest idea what he was talking about.

I explained. "He is merely pointing out that in the realm of professional basketball, Lucy, Chicago—and not New York—is the finest city in the world."

"Yep!" Jake confirmed my translation.

Suddenly Albert held up a sheet of paper he had found in one of the piles and yelled, "Look, Jake! A Neuquenormis!"

"Yep!" said Jake, examining the paper.

I realized Albert was holding up that strange bird silhouette Lucy had found in room 1502.

"Except for the feet. They got the feet wrong," Albert added.

"Yep," said Jake.

Lucy and I stared at each other in astonishment.

"What is a Neoromis?" I asked.

"A Neuquenormis," Albert corrected me. "A Mesozoic bird, Uncle Markus. Eighty-five million years ago."

"Are you sure, Albert?" Lucy asked quietly.

Jake answered for his older brother. "Yep! Albert knows everything about dinosaurs. He won two prizes."

"Dinosaurs? Wait! I thought you said this was a bird."

Albert looked at me sadly, as if my comment was so pathetic it required a saint to answer.

"Oh, Uncle Markus. Everyone knows birds are living dinosaurs."

"That is ridiculous!" I exclaimed. "Don't tell

me what birds are! I see them in the park every day."

"Calm down, Markus," Lucy said. "The boy has a point."

"What point?" I walked over and plucked the silhouette out of Albert's hand and stared at it intently.

"That's no dinosaur," I insisted.

Lucy said, "There is strong evidence that birds are the living descendants of dinosaurs."

"What evidence?"

"Anatomical similarities. And reproductive similarities. In mating, egg laying, nest construction and defense, and incubation."

"Yep!" from Jake.

Lucy gently removed the drawing and carried it to one of her large chairs. She sat down. The boys continued to rummage happily. I sat down in the chair across from her, by the window, and tried to decide if I really had the oomph to take the boys on the Circle Line. And if not, what alternative distraction could I dream up.

It shouldn't be so hard to find something else to do, I kept telling myself. While my nephews were from the Chicago suburbs and their parents were far from rubes—that still wasn't the Big Apple.

But something else kept intruding in my head. My stupid behavior. Why had I been so incredulous and downright nasty when Albert had said birds were living dinosaurs? What had happened to my scientific open-mindedness? Hadn't I spent my whole professional life in medical research? Hadn't I learned that in the world of biological phenomena, appearances mean absolutely nothing?

What an old know-nothing I must have sounded like to the young people.

Worse, to Lucy.

"Lucy!" I called out, starting to apologize.

And then I saw that she hadn't heard me . . . that her eyes were closed.

She looked pale, ill.

I rushed to her side, keeping my voice low because of the boys. "Lucy! What's the matter! Are you sick? Are you nauseous?"

I placed my palm on her brow. There was no fever.

She gently but firmly pushed my hand away.

"I'm not sick, Markus."

"But you're so pale."

"A revelation can sometimes do that."

"What revelation?"

She held up the bird silhouette.

"Markus," she said softly, "I believe we have crossed the Rubicon."

Since I had no idea what she meant, I tried a joke. "Lucy, Rex Harrison beat me out for the part. They said I was too chubby to play Caesar."

She waved the drawing at me.

"Don't you understand, Markus? Everything is falling into place."

"What?"

"The pieces."

"Pieces?"

"Pieces of Carbondale. Pieces of Markov. Pieces of death. Pieces of murder."

"All this is happening because an eleven-year-old kid says that silhouette is a prehistoric bird?"

Lucy didn't answer. I turned. My nephews were staring at us.

Lucy put her hand on my shoulder.

"I need some solitude, Markus. Just for a while. Show the young gentlemen our city. Nobody can do that better than you, you know."

Chapter 11

So I became a tour guide for three days.

After the Circle Line tour I became a whirl-wind.

I took them to the East Village and the West Village on an open double-decker bus. It was freezing.

I took them uptown to Washington Heights to visit the Museum of the American Indian. But we were told it had been closed a year before our visit, so I took a cab downtown to Bowling Green to find its most recent incarnation.

We went to a hockey game, to Coney Island, to the dinosaur extravaganza at the Museum of Natural History, and to Theodore Roosevelt's birthplace (don't ask me why).

I took them to Governors Island, the Statue

of Liberty, Ellis Island, and for all I know, Rikers Island.

I was making sure they stepped in every one of the five boroughs.

I took them to the last of the real department stores—Macy's and Bloomingdale's—and then all the athletic-wear stores, and even some thrift stores.

The place they loved the most was a comic book store on Carmine Street. That visit cost me $160 in pulp goodies.

Food didn't interest them much; as long as it was plentiful, it was satisfactory. But I took them to every ethnic variety of restaurant I could find—from Afghani (on 9th Avenue) to Senegalese (in the flower district) to Tibetan (on 3rd Avenue).

In a lovely little Filipino restaurant on 1st Avenue I had, to use Lucy's word, a revelation. And like Lucy, I couldn't really articulate the content of said revelation.

But what happened was this:

The restaurant served cafeteria-style. I sat Jake and Albert down at a table and went to the counter to select the dishes. I had been in that restaurant several times before and had grown to like the cuisine. Filipino food is hard to describe. It tastes like a synthesis of soul food and Chinese food. A lot of pork, chicken, and strange diced vegetables—all served over rice.

I brought four dishes back to the table and waited happily for their joyous response.

There was none. They didn't seem to like any of the dishes.

Piqued, I said to them that I understood quite well why they disliked the dishes, because everyone knows Filipino chefs may call it pork or chicken but the insiders know that it's really monkey meat.

Not only did they believe me but they dived into the food with gusto and proclaimed monkey meat in any of its manifestations to be superior to the Big Mac.

In short, I was a superlative tour guide for Jake and Albert, mainly because my mind wasn't on it—I was just taking them around on instinct.

It was Lucy I was thinking about and worrying about. I kept calling her. Every day. Three, four, five times a day.

And always there was that flat response and the refusal to see me on the grounds that she needed solitude.

Whatever subject I brought up—even that stupid bird drawing—elicited no response.

By the end of the third day I realized my true love might well be in the throes of a clinical depression.

So, when it was time to bring the boys to the airport for their trip home, I got there an hour early in order to get over to Lucy's as quickly as possible. I planned to discuss with her some kind of treatment—maybe Prozac or, if it was very bad, a series of the new low-voltage shock treatments, which bear no resemblance to the earlier electrocution horrors.

The airport farewell to Jake and Albert was quite nice. Because I was not waiting around to see them board, I cautioned them against checking their knapsacks. They assured me that they would not.

Then they thanked their Uncle Markus politely, as they had no doubt been coached to do.

But I grabbed them and hugged them and promised them that the next time they came to New York I would show them wonders they had never dreamed of.

By the time I got into the cab, there were tears in my eyes.

It was a hard ride back to Manhattan—a lot of traffic.

It was dark when I finally got to Lucy's place. I called from a pay phone on the corner, told her Jake and Albert were on their way home and I could be over in sixty seconds. She said, "That'll be fine, Markus."

When she opened the door I could not believe my eyes.

She was smiling. Her face was radiant. And she was wearing a long, beautifully flowing blue dress with billowy sleeves.

Right in front of me, with the door open, she then did three pirouettes, flaring the dress out as she whirled.

"Well? What do you think, Markus? Do you like it?"

"It's splendid."

"Aunt Hattie sent it to me a few months ago. It's what she wore for her second wedding. Or maybe it was the third."

"I've never seen it before."

"Of course you haven't. I never put it on before. Now stop standing there and gaping like a hound dog waiting for a soup bone. Come on in."

I stepped in, totally confused. When Lucy

starts using those down-home hound dog expressions, I always get confused.

Poor Lucy! Had I been wrong in my diagnosis of depression? Had she evolved into a *manic depressive*—this being the manic state? She certainly looked *too* happy—*too* suddenly.

She slammed the door shut then.

"Take a look!" she said, pointing to a dark bottle on one of the book stacks.

"What is it?"

"Port. Good port. Just for us, Markus."

"Since when are you a port drinker, Lucy? Since when am I?"

"Stop acting like an old man. Open that bottle!"

She kissed me on the cheek.

I walked over, picked up the bottle, and felt its weight.

"What's going on with you, Lucy?"

"Nothing at all. Just fun."

"What happened to your depression . . . your search for solitude?"

"Gone!"

"What about Carbondale? You explained to me that the reason you became pale that morning was because all the pieces were beginning to fall into place. Don't you remember?"

"Of course I remember. But that's all over now."

"Over."

"Yes. I know who the killer of Carbondale and Markov is."

My legs went watery. Still holding the bottle, I sat down heavily on one of the overstuffed chairs.

"Who?" I asked, my voice cracking.

"You'll know soon enough. I called Detective Bilboa. You do remember him, don't you, Markus? He told me he'd pick up the suspect and hold him for forty-eight hours."

"*Who is it, Lucy?!*"

"It would be very bad form to accuse anyone until the confession is obtained. But believe me, Markus, the case is closed."

"Are you telling me that little Albert revealed the murderer just by identifying that silhouette as a prehistoric bird?"

"Something like that. But remember, we were presented with clue after clue after clue. We just couldn't know at the time which was gold and which was dross."

I was becoming more and more upset. She could see it in my face.

"It's all over, Markus. Our work's finished. Let's party, as the young people say."

"No!" I barked.

She ignored my little outburst and said, "Oh, there is one little thing. A favor, Markus. Will you do me a small favor?"

I did not answer.

"There are a few loose strands. I want to clean them up for that nice Detective Bilboa. Can you go to the Turret tonight?"

"Where?"

"You know—that dance place where Genya Markov performed. Yes, tonight and tomorrow night. All you have to do is keep your eyes open and tell me if that old man shows up."

"What old man?"

"Bud Maddie. The one you bought the television set for."

"Is he the murderer?"

"Of course not. Don't be silly."

"Then why should I go there?"

"Don't press, Markus. Just do me this favor."

Then I really exploded. "Why can't you tell

me who the killer is? Why all this secrecy nonsense, Lucy? Didn't I do everything you
wanted? Didn't I help you? Didn't I introduce
you to Alfonso and take you to that bar—and
to the strip joint? Didn't I take you to
Fanelli's? And anyplace else you wanted to
go? How can you treat me this way—like a
stranger?"

"It would be unseemly for me to disclose
the murderer's name to anyone at this time.
But you'll have it within forty-eight hours, I
imagine. And I must say that you are reveal-
ing a very ungentlemanly streak, Doctor."

I leaned back in the chair and closed my
eyes, holding the port bottle against my chest.

When I opened them again I could see her
cat, Dipper, up on one of his high, high
perches, glowering at me and licking his chops
at the thought of my torn and shredded car-
cass.

"You know what I think, Lucy?"

"What?"

"I think this whole thing is an elaborate
joke. I don't think you know who the murderer is. I think you're just paying me back."

"Paying you back?"

"Yes. For something bad I did. Who knows what it was!"

"But Markus, dear, you know I'm not a vengeful person. And I don't know of anything bad that you've done lately."

"Then it's just a plain joke."

She smiled. She looked at me mysteriously. I squirmed.

Then she walked over to her writing desk, ripped a sheet of blank paper from a pad, picked up a pencil and a stapler, and returned.

"Are you still a betting man, Markus?"

"You know I like to bet on a horse once in a while."

"Yes, I know you do. So how about a wager now—with me?"

"What are we betting on, Lucy? And what are the stakes?"

"I am going to write a name on this sheet of paper. Then, after I fold it, I am going to staple it all around. Then I am going to give it to Peter Marin or John Wu tomorrow morning, for safekeeping.

"When Detective Bilboa arrests the murderer we shall open the paper up. If the name I have written down here is the name of the accused, I shall have won the bet."

"And I pay off."

"Correct, Markus. I have thought of a good payoff. You shall purchase train tickets to Quebec and two nights' lodgings at the Château Frontenac for all the members of Olmsted's Irregulars. Once there, we shall try to catch a glimpse of the extraordinarily beautiful gyrfalcon in its native habitat."

"And if the name is not the same, Lucy?"

"Why, then, I lose. And I pay off."

"And what do I get?"

She fiddled with the paper a bit. She inspected the stapler. She examined the point of her lead pencil as if to check its sharpness, although I could see even from where I sat that the point was already quite sharp.

"Here is what I shall do if I am mistaken," she said at last.

I waited.

Lucy seemed to give it a little more thought. Then she said, "If the thing is, as you say, just a bad joke, I shall check into the Plaza with you, and we shall register fictitiously as man and wife. We shall go to the movies, then for dinner—perhaps at a fancy Italian restaurant. When we return to our room I shall perform a striptease dance for you that will make the performers at the Turret seem amateurish.

"Yes, I shall be your ultimately topless and bottomless Salome. But that is only the beginning, Markus.

"From the beginning of the dance through checkout time, I will accommodate you in all the wild sinning you desire."

She stopped talking and smiled at me.

I was too flabbergasted to respond.

"Do we have a bet, Markus?"

I suddenly burst into laughter.

"What's so funny? Do you consider a weekend of wild sinning with me a humorous prospect?"

"Oh, no! No, Lucy!"

The cause of my explosive mirth was that suddenly the whole charade had become clear. Of course Lucy didn't know who the murderer was. She expected to lose. She *wanted* to lose.

Oh, the Byzantine machinations of Southern women!

What was going on was now crystal clear to me. Lucy had decided that it was time to become truly intimate with me. Since she still wasn't interested in marriage, and since her church upbringing still weighed heavily on her, she had opted for a wager. A lady pays off if she loses. Even if the payoff is "wild sinning."

All I said finally was, "Will you wear feathers during the dance?"

"Your pleasure will be my command."

"Then we have a bet," I announced.

The promise of what was to come obviously deranged me a bit and I reverted to a very old childhood custom. I held out my left pinky.

"What is this about?" Lucy asked.

"It's the way we used to seal a bet when I was a kid. Just join pinkies for a second and then pull them apart."

We did so.

"Now I must write the name."

She returned to her desk, scribbled something on the sheet of paper, folded and stapled it all around the edges.

Then she turned toward me and held it up. I nodded. She put it down on the desk very gingerly.

The ritual was oddly charming, now that I knew what the game was all about.

She walked over to me. "And now, Markus, I want you to go home, make yourself a bit raffish, and get over to the Turret like the old tomcat you are. If the old man shows up, call me and I will give you further instructions."

"But what about the port, Lucy?" I held up the bottle.

"Honestly, Markus Bloch. . . . You know I never drink port."

Once back in my apartment, I contemplated what Lucy meant by her instructions to look raffish.

Given the promise of wild sinning in the Plaza, I was going to follow all of her instructions, to the letter, and to the death if necessary.

But the only enhancement I could think of was to put on a yellow tie and hold an old hat in my hand. It was a kind of fedora.

Duke looked very morose as I headed out. He missed Albert and Jake. Let's face it—they gave him respect (for being a gangsta dog) and love. And they scratched his stomach on demand. Our relations were much less intimate.

I took a cab down to the Turret. It soon became obvious that the club's management was trying to cash in on the publicity surrounding the brutal murder of one of its stars; they had instituted a ten-dollar admission charge just to walk through the door. I paid without a fuss.

Darby, the bouncer/maître d' took me to a table. As before, he was charming and accommodating. But he gave no sign whatsoever that he recognized me.

I ordered a beer and looked around. It was crowded. And the crowd was younger than it had been the time Lucy and I were here. A number of college-age young men were in the audience, at small tables that appeared to have been pushed together in the service of a fraternity party or some such.

As for the entertainment—I was pleasantly surprised. It was a bit more sophisticated than the last time. Oh, it still featured the topless dancers and the strippers and the pounding, driving dance beat—but there was also a kind of erotic belly dancer clad in a sheer shawl edged with tinkly glass beads.

Since I now knew that this assignment was a joke, merely part of Lucy's scheme to surrender to my love for her—totally—I really didn't mind sitting there and acting as if I were on the lookout for that old lush Maddie.

I knew he wouldn't show up. And even if

he did stumble in, it wouldn't mean anything. So I sat back and enjoyed the show.

The music was a bit loud. My tie a bit tight. My hat, resting on the table, a bit outlandish. And the smoke more than a bit dense. But I really settled in, as they say. How late should I stay? There had been no instructions. Until 2:00 A.M.? That seemed sensible.

I kept turning Lucy's words over in my mind: "wild sinning." Just what were the parameters of that phrase? I got all warm and trembly. As for Lucy doing a strip for me at the Plaza? That I found a bit difficult to believe. But according to Lucy it was the linchpin of all that wild sinning.

Suddenly I had a most terrifying thought. What if Lucy had ordered me here tonight because she was going to perform? What if she had somehow wangled an opportunity to do it publicly before she did it privately—for me, her true love? It would be a kind of practice run.

But that was a ridiculous thought. I was being absurd. Still—with Lucy one never knows. She has, in fact, a streak of country eccentricity in her prim makeup that is a mile wide and sometimes just as deep.

Lucy Wayles stripping at a downtown clip joint! I couldn't get that damn thought out of my head. And, for some reason, it began to take on a frightening aspect.

What would I do if they did a drum roll and introduced the "Dixie Nightingale" and out slinked Lucy?

It was getting out of hand. I switched from beer to rye and ginger ale and turned my attention from fantasy bumps and grinds to the real-life ones being displayed on the Turret's stage.

"Round midnight," as we raffish people say, I evaluated my situation.

The girls were beginning to bore me.

There was no sight of Bud Maddie.

I was fairly besotted.

Digging deep into my right-hand pants pocket, I pulled up an assortment of coins, arranged them on the table, and, squinting in the dim light, tried to recognize a quarter. I wanted to call Lucy.

I found one after much searching, held it up, admired its form, design, and metallic makeup, carried it to the green phone booth (I don't know why it was green), and dialed my love's number.

Either she was not at home or I had called the wrong number.

Saddened, I returned to my table, gathered in all my change, left a generous tip, picked up my fedora and put it on my head, straightened my yellow tie, and with Darby's help negotiated the chairs and tables and got out of the door.

The moment I felt the crisp night air on my face I steadied and sobered.

Like a rock, I thought. I am indeed like a rock.

A derelict ambled past me.

"Bless you," he mumbled, raising his hands.

I waved back and headed toward the corner. There were no cabs in sight. I thought I smelled snow. But it wasn't even Thanksgiving yet.

"Hallo! Hallo!" The derelict who had blessed me was now stumbling back my way, greeting and blessing all animate and inanimate objects in his sight.

I could see that the poor soul cradled a huge bottle of Crazy Horse malt liquor against his chest.

"Bless you!" he cried.

"You already have," I remarked.

He stopped and, grasping the bottle by the neck, thrust it toward me.

"I've had enough," I replied. "But thank you all the same."

I tend to be very respectful of derelicts. Whether or not they are drunk. Whether or not I am drunk.

His face grew grave. He dropped the bottle. It splintered on the ground with a huge racket.

I suddenly realized that I knew this man from somewhere.

Then I saw his right hand coming toward me. I caught a glimpse of something shiny.

Instinctively, I threw up my arm.

A knife blade bit into my forearm, through my shirt and jacket. I felt a quick, fiery pain.

I shouted out something—heaven knows what—and staggered backward.

The man came toward me again.

Something emerged from the darkness—something square and black—and smashed down onto my assailant's head.

He reeled and fell to the ground.

Suddenly there were people all around me. Was I crazy? Was I dreaming?

I saw Lucy and Willa Wayne and Peter Marin and John Wu.

No, I guess I wasn't crazy. I was surrounded by Olmsted's Irregulars.

Peter pressed a folded white handkerchief against my wound.

John clucked as he picked up his laptop computer, damaged perhaps beyond repair by its contact with my attacker's skull.

The man on the ground was unconscious. An X-Acto–type knife with an aluminum handle, stained with blood—mine—lay on the ground beside him.

"And now for the envelope!" a jubilant Lucy Wayles called out.

She pulled the tiny folded paper out of her knapsack, along with a small flashlight.

She ripped the paper open, staples scattering this way and that, then shined the flashlight beam on the words written on the page.

"Please make the announcement, dear Markus."

I could see the words, but I couldn't speak. Peter read them aloud: "Don Franco."

"Turn the gentleman over," Lucy instructed John Wu.

He did. It was indeed Don Franco, Jack Wesley Carbondale's research assistant.

Lucy clapped her hands in glee like a crazed

kindergarten teacher whose class had just presented her with a batch of home-baked cookies. Then she followed with instructions to us all:

"Willa! Call 911 immediately!

"Peter! Take Markus to St. Vincent's emergency ward to get stitched up. If they ask, tell them yes, Markus has medical insurance. Then we must all get to sleep. The train to Montreal leaves at 7:56 in the morning. And thanks to dear, brave, generous Markus, we will all be aboard."

As Peter led me away, I cried out, "What is going on, Lucy?"

"It's a long train ride, Markus," she said. "There will be ample time for explanations. Now be a good boy and get your stitches. The gyrfalcons are waiting to the north."

Chapter 12

Needless to say, I was a very unhappy traveler as I sipped coffee in the lounge car hurtling toward Montreal, surrounded by my fellow birders.

My arm still hurt and throbbed in spite of the Extra Strength Tylenol I had been gobbling like M&M's.

To make matters worse, I had to shell out two hundred in cash to my building staff at six in the morning in order to persuade them to take care of Duke for three days—walks and feeding.

"Such short notice, Dr. Bloch," they had clucked. And then they held me up for two hundred dollars! Can you imagine the gall of those people?

About an hour into the ride, Lucy asked, "Well, Markus, are you up to it?"

"Up to what? Wild sinning?"

She smiled knowingly. "No. The explanation."

"I think I can handle it," I said quietly, with not a little bitterness.

"Do you want me to start at the beginning or the end of the story?"

"The end," John Wu interjected.

"I don't care where you start," I said.

"Then I'll start in the middle," she said.

Willa found that amusing. She clapped her hands. On the moving train the sound dissipated quickly.

"It was your brilliant nephew Albert who really solved this murder, Markus. When he identified that silhouette as a prehistoric bird. All the rest is, as they say, commentary."

"Give me the commentary," I said grimly.

"Of course. You see, after that identification—and keeping in mind the brutal murder of Genya Markov and the fact of all her strange costumes—I began to realize that we were not dealing with a normal type of crime.

"We were dealing with some kind of abnormality . . . some kind of madness. And here, you were most helpful, Markus."

"I?"

"Yes. With your belief that the Carbondales, man and wife, were in a folie à deux relationship. One psychotic, the other mimicking the psychosis.

"It occurred to me that there was another couple in that equation. Genya Markov and . . . someone else."

"You mean someone in the Carbondale studio other than Jack Carbondale himself?" I asked, forgetting the pain in my arm and beginning to be caught up in the accelerating story.

"Exactly. Particularly after you told me that the wounds in Markov's neck were made by some type of art studio instrument—like an X-Acto knife."

"I didn't say that, Lucy. You did."

"Yes, I did, didn't I? But you led me to that conclusion, of course. Anyway, where was I? Oh, yes. Genya Markov and someone else.

"Who could it be? Someone who shared a past with the dancer. Now, there were only three hard facts we knew about this Genya—other than that she was Jack Carbondale's playmate. One, she was at the time of her death employed as an exotic dancer. Two, she had been a ballet dancer. And three—remembering that photo on her mirror—she had been a figure skater.

"This last seemed the most plausible direction to explore."

"No one in the studio claimed to be an ice skater," I replied.

"True, Markus. But do you remember when we visited the studio and Don Franco was there, alone, looking through those cartons? Do you recall how lithe and physically fit he was for a man his age? Do you recall how well he moved? And do you recall that strange gesture he made?"

"What gesture?"

"Before he did something physical, he dropped his arms by his sides and shook his hands vigorously. That is what performers and athletes do to loosen up . . . to relax . . . before they go onstage or onto the field."

I exhaled. Sometimes Lucy was overwhelming.

She continued. "So I bet my money on Don Franco. While you were squiring your nephews about town, I put Olmsted's Irregulars on the case. Willa's husband, if you recall, is with the New York Philharmonic. He knows producers, booking agents, managers. He guided us to a promoter who handles ice shows. We ran down several casts. And we did indeed find that Don Franco had been in a professional touring company with Genya Markov.

"Then came a surprising piece of information from the manager of said company. Mr. Franco had left the company to enter a mental hospital."

She stopped speaking. I sipped the black coffee. The strong November sun was flooding the lounge car. Peter took advantage of the intermission and went to get another Danish. The train had stopped somewhere in Connecticut. When we pulled out, Lucy proceeded.

"Yes, Markus. The hunt was on. Next we utilized John's contacts. As you know, he handles the investment portfolios of several wealthy health professionals, including psychiatrists and hospital administrators. We obtained the hospital records of Mr. Franco. And what a can of worms it was!"

"'Ring of fire' would be a more apt metaphor," Peter said snidely.

"Perhaps," Lucy said. "Anyway . . . tell me,

Markus, does the phrase 'Three Christs of Ypsilanti' ring a bell?"

"Of course. It was the title of a best-selling book in the fifties."

"Do you remember what the book was about?"

"I do. Case studies of three men at a mental hospital in the Midwest. Each one believed himself to be Jesus. They were delusional, megalomaniacal psychotics. True paranoids, I believe, and not paranoid schizophrenics."

"So there you have it!"

"Have what? Are you telling me that Don Franco thought he was Christ?"

"Not Christ. Saint Francis of Assisi."

I didn't know how to respond to such a statement.

"Saint Francis," John Wu explained in that patronizing way of his. "The revered saint of Christendom who spoke to the birds."

As if I didn't know that.

"He spoke to other animals as well," Willa added.

"And we also learned, Markus, that the only other individual in the studio with a history of hospitalization for mental disorders was Bo Carbondale."

Who did she think *she* was—Saint Theresa?"
I retorted.

"No. Just Bo Carbondale. She was hospitalized for depression."

"All right, all right," I said impatiently. "But what does all this mean?"

"It meant that I finally had enough data to construct a logical sequence of events. Logical, that is, within the context of a psychotic killer."

"I don't see any sequence, Lucy."

"Ah, Markus. Be flexible. Here was the scenario I constructed. Listen carefully. Franco and Markov meet in the touring ice show. They fall in love. Franco is then hospitalized when his psychosis flares up. The psychosis is brought under control. He is released to a halfway house. He becomes friendly with another patient there—Bo Carbondale. She gets him a job in her husband's studio.

"Franco and Genya have remained lovers. She is now working at the Turret. Franco learns that Jack Carbondale is a promiscuous lecher with a liking for kinky sex. Franco skillfully insinuates Genya into Carbondale's life. She does lewd dances for him in balletic bird costumes. She slakes his erotic thirsts. Jack is bowled over. He cannot get enough of her. He will do anything for her.

"What, you may ask, was Franco's purpose in acting like a procurer, debasing the woman he supposedly loved in that way?

"Well, his purpose seems clear to me, Markus. A mad vision. He had one of his Saint Francis–type conversations with the birds and maybe with God. The birds told him they wished to be portrayed as the living descendants of the dinosaurs. They wanted this fact to be apparent in the drawings themselves. No doubt his psychosis was fueled by the enormous press coverage of new dinosaur finds each month—many of them tying the dinosaurs to birds. After all, his job was to clip and save and read these articles. He was a researcher.

"To make a long story short, Markus, under orders from the man she loved, Genya Markov persuaded Jack Wesley Carbondale to create a set of gull plates that would show the connection between birds and dinosaurs. In watercolors. A new type of Carbondale bird portrait. God knows what they looked like. Perhaps they were spectacular. Perhaps they were beautiful. Perhaps they were repellent. Perhaps the editor would have rejected them if they had ever arrived.

"But they never did. Just before the new edition of the guide was to be submitted, Jack Carbondale learned of the relationship between Franco and Genya. How he learned, I don't know. He realized he had been used by a lunatic. He felt totally betrayed by the woman he now loved.

"He destroyed the gull plates. He painted NO REMORSE on the door of the studio to show Franco that he knew what was going on and realized what a fool he had been to execute the paintings.

"Then, still raging, he went to his hotel room and waited for Genya's visit. He was going to kill her. And he was going to get his revenge in an artistic—or should I say, symbolic—way.

"He would use an ice pick because Genya had been an ice skater. He would use her dancing garter from the Turret. And he would fasten a drawing of a bird to the death instrument. It was the bird he had used to help him envision the 'dino-gull' paintings.

"But that particular murder plot was thwarted. Franco, seeing the NO REMORSE graffiti, intuited trouble. He called Genya and warned her against a visit to the Hilton. Franco turned up instead. The psychotic and the brokenhearted lecher confronted each other in room 1502. Franco demanded the plates. He didn't believe Jack had destroyed them. He had to have them published. After all, Franco received his orders from God and the birds themselves. Carbondale could not produce them. Franco flung the artist to his death.

"Then, mocking Carbondale, Franco wrote NO REMORSE on the wall.

"After this, Genya Markov finally realized her lover was beyond help and a danger to her. She tried to break the folie à deux. Franco murdered her. He brought the cartons from the studio to make it appear that he was helping her to move. He slit her throat. Never love a psychotic, Markus."

"Particularly," noted Willa, "if he thinks he's Saint Francis."

"But Saint Francis was a pacifist," said Peter Marin.

"Franco may have been psychotic, but he had a point," John said. "I believe, in fact, that depictions of birds should somehow allude to their ancestral past."

Peter shot back: "Damn it, John! Not in a bird identification guide! I want a guide to show me what a herring gull looks like *now*, not a million years ago. I don't want the evolutionary history of the gull. Or a sci-fi rendition of bird form and psyche. You're mixing apples and oranges. I don't care if birds are the last-link descendants of the dinosaurs. I don't care if they're the cousins or brothers. A gull is a gull is a gull."

"Shut up, both of you!" I shouted.

I had shocked everyone, including myself.

"Markus! What's the matter? Calm yourself," Lucy said.

"What's the matter? I'll tell you what's the matter."

I lifted my wounded arm. "You left something out of your very imaginative scenario, Lucy. You left out my being at the Turret last night—sent by you on a wild goose chase. You left out the bloody ending. The denouement."

"I was getting to it, dear. Believe me."

She patted my good arm.

"So," she went on, "having worked out that scenario, I laid a bit of a trap."

"It's illegal to trap butcher birds," I said, always ready with a quip, even when in extremis.

Lucy smiled her wonderful smile.

Then she dug into her knapsack, retrieved a small object, and handed it to me.

It was a matchbox from the Turret. I remembered when she had taken some from the table.

"Open it, Markus."

I obeyed. There was a piece of paper inside, folded to a fare-thee-well.

I opened it and smoothed it out.

The page was essentially a photocopy of the bird silhouette. But in bold Magic Marker along the side of the silhouette was the note "$50,000 IN CASH WILL BE THE PRICE OF MY SILENCE."

I looked up, confused.

"I delivered that message—anonymously, of course—in that matchbox to each of Carbondale's associates. The killer, I knew, would have to silence the sender. Of course, I knew who the killer was by then. But I sent one to all the assistants. After all, I *do* make mistakes."

I felt as if I had been slammed in the face with a large wet towel.

"My God, Lucy! You sent me into a trap! I could have been killed. You used me as live bait!"

"We were in the area with you all the time, Markus. Hidden. Backing you up. We did get to the actual scene a tad late. But then again, we had to wait until he used the weapon against you . . . the same weapon that he used on Genya Markov."

She sat down beside me then. She stroked my face.

"Besides," Lucy said, "everyone knows you are the bravest soul in Olmsted's Irregulars."

No one spoke for a long time. I closed my eyes and listened to the hum of the wheels on the rails.

The closeness of Lucy, the lull of the train, even the throbbing in my arm, suddenly, in concert, raised my spirits.

I thought of all that wild sinning that had eluded my grasp. But . . . there were many hours left to this ride. The compartments were private. I turned, expectantly, to Lucy.

She was staring out the window with a beatific look on her face.

My spirits plunged as quickly as they had risen. I knew what she was thinking of: a long-winged gyrfalcon flying fast and low in its white-plumed splendor.

Oh, it was going to be cold on the tundra.

Besides, I didn't deserve any wild sinning. I had lost the bet. And I am, if nothing else, a good loser.

An excerpt from the next Lucy Wayles mystery

My father, may he rest in peace, used to say that there are three topics that should never be brought up at dinner. Or breakfast or lunch for that matter: sex, politics, and religion.

He left out birds.

Predictably, it was the subject of birds that started the argument on that very warm August morning.

It was about 10:30.

We—and by "we" I mean the Olmsted's Irregulars—had just spent three hours or so bird watching in the Ramble, that thickly wooded gem in Central Park.

There were six of us—

Lucy Wayles, the founder, spiritual adviser, and master sergeant of our group.

Peter Marin, a charter member, a large red-haired man who, though he dresses and looks like a bearded Li'l Abner, is in fact a successful and highly regarded commercial artist with an astonishing triplex apartment.

John Wu, another charter member, slim and fastidious, an investment counselor who lives and dies by his laptop, on which he accomplishes all kinds of byzantine trading and the mysterious manipulation of even more mysterious data.

Myself, Markus Bloch, also a charter member. I am a retired M.D.—a medical researcher known primarily as the man who loves Lucy Wayles and follows her about like Sancho Panza.

Two of our number are new to the group, making up for the departure of the lovely Willa Wayne, who had to leave us when her husband, a violinist with the New York Philharmonic, secured a second chair position with the Cleveland Orchestra.

Timothy (last name not revealed) is a tall, gangly, excruciatingly shy young black man with the largest feet I have ever seen on a human. He is a science-fiction writer, a waiter by night, and a diligent birder. We all like Timothy, but once in a while he behaves in a peculiar fashion. He is constantly becoming perplexed about arcane matters that have nothing to do with the matter at hand—i.e., bird watching. You might be next to him in a glade, binoculars raised, and you'll hear him mutter something like, "I cannot *believe* that there are really seven thousand islands in the Philippines."

The second new member is Isobel Soba, a jolly, heavy-set former Maryknoll nun who now teaches in the graduate center of Fordham University. Lucy, when she was still director of the Library of Urban Natural History (since absorbed by the Museum of Natural History), had met Isobel at some kind of professional gathering and suggested that she join a bird watching group. So she did, belatedly. Isobel has a few personal quirks—habits, problems, however you'd like to put it—that the rest of the group found difficult to bear at first. She smokes, for one;

in fact, she chain smokes an evil-smelling low tar menthol cigarette. She is also the only birder I ever came across who, in the summer, goes birding with a portable ice chest to hold her cans of beer. She favors a strange imported brew, unknown to me, and she seems to consume it by the barrel. But all that was soon overcome, since she is a joy to be with. The one lingering area of mistrust vis à vis Isobel was a troubling rumor that she was a tree hugger . . . that she was seen hugging a European beech just past the Bow Bridge. But Lucy assured us that if indeed Isobel was a tree hugger, she was not the kind that hated woodpeckers.

So, that is the cast of characters, so to speak.

Now, let me get to the argument.

We were all weary when we climbed down the small gully where we always took our repast. Quickly, out came the hard-boiled eggs and the oranges and the bottles of spring water.

It had been a very busy morning for bird watchers. The late summer migration out of the park was starting. The social birds were restless . . . always moving . . . gathering into flocks. The solitaries seemed to be praying.

At one point early on in the morning—we were in the Ramble at the time—John Wu had casually announced that he had spotted a yellow-breasted chat.

"Where?" Lucy asked, in that throaty whisper all serious birders cultivate.

"Over there, in the brush, behind the stone arch. But he's gone," John said. And the sighting was forgotten even though it is rare to see a yellow-breasted chat in Central Park.

It was not until some hours later, as we were resting and eating, that Isobel, one of the new Irregulars, said rather sternly to John, "Are you sure it was a yellow-breasted chat you saw?"

All the old timers tensed. Of all the wrong things you might say to John Wu, challenging one of his pronouncements was about the "wrongest" you could possibly get.

John continued with the peeling of his second hard-boiled egg, finishing the task before he responded to Isobel with an arch "Excuse me?"

Isobel lit one of her cigarettes and blew the smoke skyward. "Well, all I'm saying is that it's odd that no one else saw it. We were all bunched together."

"The bird was skulking," John explained.

For some reason Isobel found this very funny. She burst out laughing at the talk of the skulking bird.

John opened a napkin, laid it on the grass, placed the stripped egg on the napkin, and stared at the new member of the group. I experienced a small but measurable shudder of fear. I looked to Lucy for help or corroboration. She seemed uninterested. She seemed, in fact, utterly absorbed in her orange, having done with the peeling and now moving on to sectioning it. I sighed. Everything about that woman fascinated me. Even the way she peeled an orange. That, dear children, is love among the older set. It has its own peculiarities.

But then I caught her giving John Wu a quick,

ever so quick and anxious glance. As head of the Olmsted's Irregulars, she knew her troops as well as she knew the park's birds, and sometimes John Wu spiraled out of control.

"My dear lady," John Wu said, lapsing into the kind of formal address that was an unmistakable signal of his irritation, "the yellow-breasted chat is one of the largest of the warblers. It has many un-warbler-like characteristics . . . such as singing like a mockingbird. It does not really behave or look like a warbler at all. But it *is* one. I assure you I know it when I see it. And I saw it skulking in the Ramble."

Miss Isobel Soba listened, grinned, popped a can of her strange beer and went into a Tallulah imitation: "Dahling! If you say chat . . . I say chat." She then began to puff furiously at her ciga-rette, drawing in and blowing out absurd amounts of smoke and holding onto the filter tip as if it were one of those vampish, bejeweled holders from the 1920s.

This really infuriated John, but before he could retaliate, Peter Marin said the three little words that ended the argument.

"I'm getting married," he announced.

There was stunned silence.

"The day after tomorrow," Peter continued. "Right here. Where we are now standing—or sit-ting, as the case may be. And you're all invited. There'll be a party at my place afterward . . . just for the Olmsted's Irregulars . . . and there'll be more good food than you ever saw in your life. And two bands. And hand-dipped ice cream from . . .

from . . . well, somewhere in New Jersey, with a barrel of crushed walnuts in syrup."

"Congratulations, Peter," Lucy said, firmly. Then added, "Would it be possible to find out whom you are marrying before the ceremony?"

"Oh yes indeed! Her name is Teresa Aguilar. And she is the most beautiful and intelligent and exciting woman I have ever met. You will all love her. And she'll love you."

All kinds of cryptic glances were being thrown about. Because those who knew Peter Marin knew that when it came to women, he was a demented middle-aged bachelor. He fell in and out of love with great rapidity and great intensity—virtually always with the most inappropriate partners, such as fanatical cult members or cross dressers.

Lucy asked sweetly, "Do I know her, Peter?"

"I don't think so. I just didn't bring her around. But once we're married you'll see her all the time. She loves the park. She loves birds. She loves people."

Peter thumped the ground beside him. "And . . . can you imagine? . . . we have decided to get married right here."

Timothy, who was stretched out on the grass, feet toward the small rivulet which bisected the gully, offered Peter one of his peanut butter crackers. Peter waved it off.

"I thought it would be perfect. Come as you are. We finish birding for the morning and then we just have a wedding. Mine. Lucy! Don't you think it's a brilliant idea?"

"Brilliant!" Lucy agreed.

"Rain or shine," Peter said. "Two days from now. Right here. Same time, same station. It will be as if nothing was planned. Like a good sketch-book."

The skulking yellow-breasted chat was now only a dim memory.

I took out my black plastic Glad bag—entrusted to me because I was official garbage person for the Olmsted's Irregulars—and began a preliminary clean-up.

I could hear John Wu telling Peter that he should reconsider this marital step. "I don't believe you have thought it through," he was saying.

When Isobel Soba said, "Amen!" John gave her a dirty look. She blew smoke at him. I took a misstep and a spasm of pain shot through my lower back. I yelped, turned, and groaned. Lucy was looking at me with concern.

I smiled to show her it was just a twinge. She smiled back. My heart fair to burst to see my true love so lovely and so regal and so compassionate in that gully. Oh Lucy Wayles . . . she had that kind of severe mature beauty leavened with a smidgen of depravity . . . if I may use that word.

Then Lucy did a very strange thing. She winked at me. I had no idea what it meant. So I just went back to my assignment and completed it to the best of my ability.

The funny thing was, it happened just as Peter Marin said it would happen and it didn't seem strange at all.

Furthermore, from the time Peter announced it to the time the actual event commenced . . . nobody even spoke about it.

No doubt, most of us didn't think it would happen. This was not the first time Peter Marin had announced wedding plans.

But there we were. In the gully again, resting, peeling hard-boiled eggs and oranges.

It was a cooler and darker morning and the birding had been poor.

Everyone, including Peter, was dressed in the usual manner for a field trip.

Then . . . what a transformation.

A beautiful woman in a white dress with a white shawl appeared on the rim of the gully.

Accompanying her, his arm carefully linked with hers, was a kindly-looking man in a brown suit. Last, there was a younger man carrying a collapsible table and several bottles of champagne.

Timothy whispered to me, "We have now reached one of the outermost planets in the galaxy."

Teresa Aguilar, Peter Marin's intended, made her way down the slope. As crazy as the unfolding scene was, I felt a sudden and bitter pang of jealousy. If only that were Lucy Wayles coming down that slope to take my hand . . . "to be joined forever in the bosom of the Lord," as her mad old Aunt Hattie would say (forgive me, Spinoza).

Peter guided his beloved around the gully, introducing her to each of the Olmsted's Irregulars.

She was a small, sweet-looking thing . . . very

slim . . . with one of those swanlike Spanish necks. Her jet black hair was cut short, and the white shawl around her shoulders combined with the white dress made her seem like an angel sent down from above on some specially lovely mission.

When the champagne bottles were judiciously lined up for the eventual uncorking, and the brown-suited gentleman, who, Peter told us, was a Unitarian minister, had taken his place behind the now opened table—we all knew this was no joke. This *was* a marriage. Peter Marin was really about to get married.

They made a very odd couple as they approached the table.

She, so young and so beautiful and so elegant.

He, so burly and crazed looking in his Li'l Abner coveralls and his red beard.

I said to Lucy, "He certainly picked a beautiful young lady to marry."

For some odd reason this comment irked her. I could tell she was irked because she started to snap the old hippie headband that she always wore when birding. And then, as if to prove beyond a shadow of a doubt that she was indeed angry at my innocent remark, she snapped her binocular case shut.

"Dear, sweet Markus," she said with a kind of indulgent sigh. This was another Southern down-home affectation she often used to make a point. "Remember the white-eared hummingbird."

She patted my arm for emphasis.

Oh no. Another one of her infuriating cryptic sayings.

"What does that mean, Lucy?" I demanded in a hushed whisper, my eyes on the bride and groom.

"Leks," said John Wu.

"What?" I said.

"Is that a soup?" Isobel Soba queried.

"No!" snapped John. "A lek is a site on which male birds display communally to attract females. The white-eared hummingbird males sing all together. The female struts by and chooses the one who sings best, then leads him away to mate."

"But Lucy," I said, "Peter Marin's voice is even worse than mine."

Lucy gave me a withering look. Obviously I had, once again, missed the point.

Isobel hushed us. The ceremony was about to begin.

The minister placed a tooled leather Bible on the table along with two gold rings.

He looked benevolently at the bride and groom; he looked out at the guests.

"We are about to embark on what is, in my opinion, the most sacred ritual in Christendom," he said. "The binding of two souls in holy matrimony."

He paused thoughtfully then. "Did it ever occur to you why the harsh word 'binding'—which has its Old Testament origins in the binding of Isaac for sacrifice—is also used for the marriage ceremony?"

He began to explain.

But a sudden shout from above stopped him.

A rollerblader on the West Drive had obviously gotten into difficulty, lost control, jumped the small barrier, and was now hurtling down the gully toward us.

The young skater, a long-haired blond, was holding on to his helmet with both hands and screaming out warnings.

The grass gully slowed the rollerblader down and he stumbled to a halt right beside the minister's table.

He pulled the helmet off and laughed heartily. We all joined in the laughter.

He pointed to the Bible on the table. "Divine intervention," he said, obviously in explanation of his miraculous trip down the gully, unscathed and standing.

Indeed, we were still laughing when he pulled a small, smoke gray handgun from inside his helmet, pressed it flush against the bride's temple, and pulled the trigger.

The sound of death is paralyzing. It was impossible to move. We might have all been rocks.

Teresa Aguilar fell over the table.

The rollerblader kicked off his skates, tucked them under his arm, ran up the slope and vaulted over the wall onto Central Park West.

I could see clearly the Bible stained with the bride's blood and gore.

For some reason, two thoughts crossed my mind.

The first one was irrational: I recalled that the title of Edmund Wilson's great work on the Civil War—*Patriotic Gore*—came from the song "Oh Maryland, My Maryland."

The second thought was quite rational. Pity, I said to myself, there'll be no wedding this morning.

If you enjoyed this
Lucy Wayles mystery,
be sure to read the
following books in the
Dr. Nightingale series

DR. NIGHTINGALE
COMES HOME

Deirdre "Didi" Quinn Nightingale needs to solve a baffling mystery to save her struggling veterinary practice in New York state. Bouncing her red jeep along country roads, she is headed for the herd of beautiful, but suddenly very crazy, French Alpine dairy goats of a "new money" gentleman farmer. Diagnosing the goats' strange malady will test her investigative skills and win her a much needed wealthy client. But the goat enigma is just a warm-up for murder. Old Dick Obey, her dearest friend since she opened her office, is found dead, mutilated by wild dogs. Or so the local police force says. Didi's look at the evidence from a vet's perspective convinces her the killer species isn't canine but human. Now she's snooping among the region's forgotten farms and tiny hamlets, where a pretty sleuth had better tread carefully on a twisted trail of animal tracks, human lies, and passions gone deadly . . .

DR. NIGHTINGALE
RIDES THE ELEPHANT

Excitement is making Deirdre "Didi" Nightingale, D.V.M., feel like a child again. There'll be no sick cows today. No clinic. No rounds. She is going to the circus. But shortly after she becomes veterinarian on call for a small traveling circus, Dolly, an extremely gentle Asian elephant, goes berserk and kills a beautiful dancer before a horrified crowd. Branded a rogue, Dolly seems doomed, and in Didi's opinion it's a bum rap that shouldn't happen to a dog. Didi is certain someone tampered with the elephant and is determined to save the magnificent beast from being put down. Her investigation into the tragedy leads her to another corpse, an explosively angry tiger trainer, and a "little people" performer with a big clue. Now, in the exotic world of the Big Top, Didi is walking the high wire between danger and compassion . . . knowing that the wild things are really found in the darkness, deep in a killer's twisted mind.

DR. NIGHTINGALE GOES TO THE DOGS

Veterinarian Deirdre "Didi" Quinn Nightingale has the birthday blues. It's her day, and it's been a disaster. First she's knee-deep in mud during a "bedside" visit to a stud pig. Then she's over her head in murder when she finds ninety-year-old Mary Hyndman shot to death at her rural upstate farm.

The discovery leaves Deirdre bone-weary and still facing Mary's last request: to deliver a donation to Alsatian House, a Hudson River monastery famous for its German shepherds. Deirdre finds the retreat filled with happy dogs, smiling monks, and peace.

This spur-of-the-moment vacation rejuvenates Deirdre's flagging strength and spirit until another murder tugs on her new leash on life. Deirdre's investigative skills tell her this death is linked to Mary's. But getting her teeth into this case may prove too tough for even a dauntless D.V.M. . . . when a killer with feral instincts brings her a hairsbreadth from death.

DR. NIGHTINGALE
GOES THE DISTANCE

Intending to forget about her sick cats and ailing cows for one night, Deirdre "Didi" Quinn Nightingale, D.V.M., is all dressed up for a champagne-sipping pre-race gala at a posh thoroughbred farm. She never expects death to be on the guest list while hobnobbing with the horsey set and waiting to meet the famous equine vet, Sam Hull. But when two shots ring out, two bodies lie in the stall of the year's most promising filly.

The renowned Dr. Hull is beyond help, and the filly's distraught owner offers Didi a fee and a thoroughbred all her own to find this killer. Now Deirdre is off snooping in a world of bloodlines, blood money, and bloody schemes. The odds are against this spunky vet who may find that her heart's desire is at stake—and murder waiting at the finish line . . .